Aïkóna

Taming The Impostor Saga Book ii

Adventure Time Travel Fantasy Series
For the young at heart.

Sheri Vie

Doctor Vie Publications

Δἵκόnἂ version 1.0

Copyright © 2017 by Dr. Sheri Vie

Δἵκόnἂ may be ordered through booksellers or by contacting:
Doctor Vie Publications
www.DrVie.com/contact
***

First printing February 2017 in the USA
eISBN: 978-1-988705-04-0
ISBN Paperback: 978-1-988705-01-9
ISBN Audiobook: 978-1-988705-07-1

Special Gifts for You

Especially for You

Want to learn about the African setting for the series?
Go to <u>DrVie.com/</u> <u>Taming-The-Impostor-map</u>

FREE SHORT STORY FOR YOU

<u>DrVie.com/VIPfreebooks</u>

Prequel to Taming The Impostor Saga

ᴅïκónᴀ **dedication**

Honors my dearest **Mom**, who supports and accompanies me on many of the "back-routes" featured in Taming the Impostor Saga.

***

And in reverence to:
The memory of my dearest **Dad,** who piqued my love for adventure, which catalyzed the characters, and to
the memory of my dearest **Grandma**, and her fascinating stories of superpowers and Utopian legends, sprinkled throughout the Saga.

***

And recently
In memory of my dear friend **Michael-Sean O'Connell**, passed at age 29 on 7 January 2017, who at my side in 2016, encountered a young boy in South Africa, who inspired the character of Siya

CONTENTS

CHAPTER ONE

Leaving Giant's Castle

Day Zero Continued

TWIGS CRACKLED, BIRDS fluttered, and trees groaned in the dark forest of the Draco mountains.

Inside the stony cave high in Giant's Castle, Shiana, Siya, and Jali draped themselves on the cold walls, and Brelize hid her red tail behind Meosic's thick sandy fur. The young prince's bright halo of fireflies flickered and dimmed and his pointed ears twitched.

All gazes fixed on the grotto's dense fern doorway.

It ripped open.

A tall figure occupied the entrance.

Its long coat swayed in the still night, ushering in an icy blast of air, sending shivers up Jali's neck.

Surfing on a crescendo of waves, its voice crashed off the jagged rocks. "Ms. Kriaka, it's me, Pierre."

Erratic sounds flooded the cave and jarred Jali's heart. He tried to remain calm as Rama and Kriaka emerged out of the shadows.

Pierre advanced toward them, his unlit face indistinguishable from the surroundings. "I followed you from the meeting." The man waited for a response before continuing. "Look, word is spreading that the Dragons know of your plan to find the GIFT. They're advancing this way. I came to warn you."

At the mention of the Dragons, Jali shuddered. His uneasiness worsened when Herby left his side and joined Rama. The two men brushed past Pierre and peered outside. A rumble echoed in the distance.

In a swift motion, the man towered over Kriaka. "They've assembled Dragon Dogs. You must leave at once."

Jali felt Shiana's grip tighten on his arm, and next to him Siya stifled a gasp.

"Where can we go Rama?" Kriaka's voice appeared laden with fear.

"You know our place near Cathedral Peak? We cut across the mountains to Sherman's Cave," Rama said, as he and Herby rushed back in.

"Agreed."

Herby hastily gathered their bags and motioned to the youngsters who edged out from the shadows.

Pierre darted a look at them and back to the trio. "Rama, your jalopy's not up to a fast ride. What do you think?"

Rama tugged at his cap and scratched his bearded chin. "Hmmm. Ja, bru. Best to split up, throw them off our trail. Why not take Kriaka, Shiana, and Siya through the old highway?"

Meosic leaped into Shiana's arms, but Pierre's attention seemed focused on Jali, who sauntered behind Siya. "Say, who's the Halloween kid?"

Jali pulled his Earth-boy hood close over his eyes and ears before Herby interjected. "He's a friend of Siya's from the US."

Rama helped to further deflect the interrogation. "Come on, no time to lose."

They scattered from the cave, following Pierre's fast hike off the mountain plateau. Jali wavered. It would be his first proper exploration of Earth's surroundings since the Dragons' attack on him. He winked at the creeping ferns, violet flowers, and green and purple forest rain frogs hovering in the milieu. *Thanks for supporting my recovery and thermo regulation.*

Rama's guiding hand on his shoulders propelled him, as he left the only haven he had known since becoming stranded on the foreign planet earlier in the day.

3

The steep trail lit with fireflies, meandered down through the tropical forest. He spared a quick glance at the blue copper butterflies and his ears perked at their farewells. "Bye, Prince Jali."

Waving back, he smiled. *I am finally on my adventure.*

At the foot of the trail, Pierre accompanied Shiana and Siya to a low red shuttle in front of a larger black one—smaller than the one from which the Dragons had attacked him.

From behind the larger shuttle, Rama shouted to Pierre, "It should take us two to three hours to rendezvous at Sherman's Cave. Kriaka knows the way. She'll guide you!"

"Sounds like a plan," Pierre said. He smiled at Kriaka.

Herby stacked the rest of bags in the back of the long shuttle. Jali was trying to process the scene with the strange transport systems, when the doctor tapped him.

"What's the matter, Prince Jali?"

His obvious reluctance must have revealed his confusion, prompting empathy from Herby.

"It's okay, Prince Jali, these are the smaller cars and bigger trucks we use here to get around. You know, to transport us." He opened the back door of the truck. "See, you sit in there." He guided him inside. "Once we get going, you can ask all you want, okay?"

Jali agreed. He sank into the soft cloth seat, and immediately wrinkled his nose. *What is that smell?*

Herby chuckled at his sign of distaste. "Ja, what can I say? Here, let me open the windows for some fresh air."

Rama, already in the driver seat, hurried them. "Come on, you guys, what's takin' so long?"

The vehicle jerked. Jali coughed, and covered his nose. *What a horrid smell.*

Herby, seated next to Rama, turned around and shrugged. "Ah, Prince Jali, sorry. Welcome to our polluted world."

Jali scanned the truck and analyzed as much as possible, before it jolted into motion to follow the car ahead of them. Shiana and Siya waved to him, and the sand cat jumped up and meowed. *Where is Brelize?*

He bumped around on the seat in immense discomfort, his ears hurting from the continuous noise emitted by both vehicles. *Oh no, this truck does not fly!* Instead it appeared to drag on the ground, crushing an assortment of creamy yellow plants and small shrubs in its way. Reaching out the window he tried to apologize to the distraught flora, and reeled when Brelize jumped in and landed on his lap.

"There you are!" he said. Her squirrel face smiled, and the long red hairs on her furry back bopped as she hurtled along the seat on their rough ride.

Rama turned. "Hey, kid, not a good idea, shoving your hands out the window. Best to keep 'em inside, especially at night."

"Ja, Prince Jali," Herby agreed. "You'll be safer that way. And by the way, I forgot to introduce you to our loyal transport bakkie. We call her Jen," he said, and stroked the ceiling.

Jali mimicked the doctor's actions, while struggling to adjust to the rough ride. "Hello, Jen."

The men laughed with apparent amusement.

Herby quieted and within a few moments, his face stiffened. "I don't smaak the way that Pierre guy eyes Kri."

Rama maneuvered Jen through the narrow path and chuckled. "Chill out, bru this guy is helping us." Rama pointed. "Just off this section, and we'll see our friend the old man at the boom gates."

He swung Jen, and sent Jali and Brelize hurling across to the window.

"Prince!" she shouted.

Jali caught the tip of her long tail halfway out the truck and cradled her shivering body.

Ahead of them Pierre's car raced past a dimly lit raised boom gate.

Herby craned his neck. "Where's the old fella?"

But the deserted area revealed neither an old man

nor any activity. A damaged rectangular container lay on the side of the exit.

"Look, the petrol tank!" Rama pointed. "Shoot, man, I think the Dragons got him!"

At the mention of the violent Dragons, Jali's mouth dried, and he distracted the memory willfully, with the help of his new-found friend. Supposedly tired of being flung around, she ran up his jacket, and nestled in the safety of his Earth-boy hood. The foursome sped behind Pierre up a winding path through the darkened mountains. From below, the rush of a creek reverberated through the pass.

They journeyed in silence, until Rama screeched to a halt behind the car. "We part ways here and meet up at Sherman's Cave."

Herby leaned out the window and waved at the car turning right, and Kriaka, Shiana, and Siya waved back. Jali returned their waves, and the two vehicles traveled in opposite directions.

"Fast car," Rama said, his arm resting on the open window. "They'll be there way before us."

Herby grunted and appeared troubled. "Where'd he come from, this rich ho, Pierre?"

Rama smacked the doctor's knee. "Jealous, bru?" He sneered. "You should know better than to think my sis will fall for a guy like that! She adores you, man. Why do you think she didn't go back to the US?"

Herby fiddled with his shirt. "Ja, I reckon. But that Pierre, he's too smart, too trendy, and too good-looking, man—"

"Snap out of it, Herby," Rama said. He continued in a gentler tone. "Look, we've come this far, and Kri is obsessed with getting the kid back home." He darted a quick glance at Jali. "The sooner I get this done the better." He rapped on the steering wheel. "The First Ones should have feedback on the GIFT soon. We got a lot to do, man, to find the GIFT."

Herby poked his head in the back. "How you feeling, Prince Jali?" A concerned smile filled the doctor's fair face and his blue eyes sparkled with kindness.

Jali relaxed, feeling comforted by his soft voice. "I am well, thank you, Doctor Herby."

As they accustomed to the bumpy road, Brelize returned to the seat, stretched in comfort, and curled her tail around his wrist.

He adjusted the Earth-boy jacket that Kriaka had given him, hiding his Third Eye and pointed ears. He smiled with delight. *Now I look like them.*

Rama extended his hand out of the window. "Great thing that it's a cool summer night, let's hope it keeps up." He peered at Jali. "You gotta hang in there, kiddo, it sure as heck stinks when you're stuck in the wrong place at the wrong time."

He slammed his hand on the wheel and turned to Herby. "Can you imagine what the Dragons would've done if they found him first? Thank our lucky stars for our little Siya." He cleared the long hair from the back of his neck, and nodded.

Jali's Third Eye fluttered, and a tingle ran up his spine, lodging itself in between his emerald eyes. His pointed ears perked, before he blurted, "Turn left, Rama Adi. We must avoid the Dragons who await us farther along this path."

❊ ❊ ❊ ❊ ❊ ❊

CHAPTER TWO

STRANDED

THE DOCTOR MOANED.

Rama reeled to the back. "How do you know about the roadblock, kid?"

Jali stared ahead, and replied in a monotone. "I see them, I hear them."

"Oh man, in the dead of night, and you see them and hear them? Yeah, right! Well, we don't see anyone."

Despite his warning, they proceeded, and bumped over the endless holes in the gritty road.

"How can you be sure, Prince Jali?" the doctor's soft voice prompted.

His Third Eye fluttered under the hood and he spoke in a steady voice. "Three trucks larger than Jen, five armed men are positioned on the top. Cars like Pierre's, flashing red lights. A sign reads Escort."

"Oh, man!" Rama said. The truck screeched to a halt.

Brelize skidded to the floor, but Jali remained in his trance-like state.

"Look Rama, I think we should listen to Prince Jali. How else could he know the road sign a kilometer away?"

Rama motioned to the back, his voice raised. "And the left turn back there, where does that go? It seems to be heading through the tribal villages, the no-man's-land!"

Jali's Third Eye fluttered, and with his ears perked he continued to describe his visions. "Rama Adi, the bulky Dragon on the side of the truck says, 'Caution all riot squads, be on the look out for the Brown Witch, Mr. Hyde, and Doctor Jekyll. They are armed and dangerous. Shoot to destroy.'"

"Prince Jali," Herby said. "How did you know our code names? Only the secret First Ones know that."

His ears relaxed, and his Third Eye closed. "I can hear them and see them!" He grinned with delight. "Graduates of Level-4 have these abilities on Zooka."

I have super-vision, I have super-vision finally!

"Okay, look, Rama, we can cut through the back of the tribal villages, avoid the road block, and still rendezvous," Herby said. "If Kri was here, she'd say the same."

"I don't believe I'm listening to a kid!" Rama yelled.

He swung Jen, and they journeyed back.

Herby looked at Jali and winked.

Jali smiled, feeling energized. *My superpower is on, I'm an Earth boy with superpowers. Reena and Grandma will be proud of me!* He drew his Earth-boy hood firmly over his head and stroked Brelize's back.

Within a short distance the thick forest revealed a narrow passageway, through which Rama threaded Jen. Herby heaved himself through his window, and hanging on the side he reported on the dark surroundings. They proceeded with attention, their eyes and ears alert for ambushes. Jen continued without incident for some time.

"Stop," Herby whispered.

Rama slowed the truck to a halt. He held on to the top of the window and heaved his body through the truck.

"I knew it!" he said. "It's those tribal warriors. Told you they prowl at night!" The men discussed their next move as they sank back in their seats. "Oh man, we better avoid those guys. You know what they did to the lot who got lost here!" Rama said. He twisted to the back and reversed Jen.

Jali's ears perked. "Look!" He pointed to the white plumes pouring from the front of the truck.

"Darn, Jen, don't let me down now. Not now, Jen!" Rama said.

"We better check her out, else we'll lose her," Herby said.

Rama stopped and shook his head, his voice steeped in frustration. "Shoot, man!"

The two men ventured out to investigate the damage. Rama opened the front cover of the truck, and they jumped back as a shot of white vapors gushed up in the dark forest. "We're busted, man. Jen's heating up."

Jali tiptoed to their side. *This might not be as bad as they think.* "Can you recharge Jen and heal her?"

Rama sneered; he paced to and fro.

Jali squinted, trying to understand the severity of the situation. *Life on this planet is different from home. I think the beings here are unable to regenerate injury.*

Herby walked around the truck and scanned the area. "Look, we have no choice but to hope for help from one of the tribal villages."

"Heh, you crazy, man? Who knows what they do there, grind our bones for muthi?"

The two men sank on the grass alongside Jen, deep in thought. Jali and Brelize joined them, as fireflies flitted above.

Rama jumped up. "You're right, bru, that's our only bet. I'll go. You watch the kid and Jen."

Herby rose. "No way. Do you think the tribe will show mercy to a calm white guy or a crazy unshaven

Indian guy with anger issues?"

Rama glared at him.

But Herby ignored him. "Look, I've dealt a lot with the African tribes at the medical clinic. Who knows, maybe they'll recognize me. Why not I go? I'll be less risky there."

Rama shuffled, and huffed and puffed.

Herby accepted his fussing as consent. "Keep him in check, Prince Jali, and stay out of sight." He readjusted Jali's hood, shook Rama's hand, and vanished into the forest.

Rama beckoned Jali to sit with him at a large tree trunk, and Brelize scampered with.

"Can you see what is happening out there, kid?" Rama asked, resting his back against the trunk.

He shook his head in dismay. "Rama Adi, I find that I have recently acquired the superpower of my Third Eye. For now it appears to synchronize with my super-hearing when I am threatened. I am unable to predict much more."

Rama clasped his head and sighed. "Just our luck!" He turned to where the doctor had left for help. "Man, I hope they don't make poor Herby into muthi."

Jali cocked his head to one side. "What is muthi, Rama Adi?"

He chuckled and quickly muffled his laughter. "Oh

kid, you don't wanna know."

"Yes, Rama Adi, I want to learn."

"Okay, kid, here it is. You see, in a few places across the border, it's believed that some people use black magic—ya know, witchcraft—to cast spells over others. At times they sneak across here to collect body parts to mix into a potion, muthi, and call in the supernatural powers."

"Brown Witch," Jali said. "Why did the Dragons call Kriaka Adi the Brown Witch? Does she make the muthi?"

Rama rapped him gently on his hood. "Heck no, kid. Let me tell you about our Kri." He propped himself on one knee and twiddled a twig. "When she came home to bury our parents, for some odd reason those Dragons feared her." He coughed and snapped the twig.

"Kriaka Adi is kind."

"Yeah, yeah, kid. We call her Mother Nature. She's always close to nature. From a teeny tot, hanging out in the woods and forests. You know, a month after the burial, Herby found her in the back garden, unconscious. When she came to, she said she could sense that something bad was happening to Earth and we must prepare to save the best of our planet." He ripped off his cap and rubbed his face. "She's my little sis. My only family. I will protect her, and I'll destroy all those monsters who killed our parents, and my Jenni." His voice choked and he got up and strode into the forest.

Jali's felt a painful emptiness deep inside. He missed his Mama and Papa, whom he had never seen. Why did people die before their time? As he leaned against the tree trunk with his friend Brelize at his side, he sighed, sharing the pain of which Rama spoke.

Suddenly, his ears perked.

What was that?

❄ ❄ ❄ ❄ ❄ ❄

CHAPTER THREE

Captured

JALI SPRANG UP and with Brelize at his heels, wandered in the direction of the shouts. A short distance into the forest, he crawled and crouched behind the low bushes in front of him.

A group of ten dark-skinned male warriors, with spears and shields, surrounded Rama. A few carried fire sticks. Rama extended his hands in the air and fell to his knees.

Jali's heart pounded. He molded himself into the trees and silenced his breath.

Brelize scurried high up a branch to rally help from nearby squirrels.

Ahead of them, the warriors dragged Rama through the shadows of the fire-lit forest. Jali darted in and out of the woods, his newly acquired troop of squirrels following close, their way brightened by fireflies.

A muffled groan echoed toward them. *Doctor Herby!*

Near a short mud dwelling with a triangular thatched roof, the men flung Rama alongside the doctor, whose hands were tied behind his back. Fire sticks planted in the ground, tossed snakes of brightness on the clearing. The warriors raised their spears high and danced around the prisoners, just as Siya had done in the cave, their skin and hair the same as Siya's. Their narrow hips clothed with short loin cloths, and their wrists and ankles adorned with bracelets. Two warriors tied Rama's hands, and gagged the men's mouths.

The small army circled their captives. Jali's ears perked and his hearing tuned in to their chatter. They deliberated about the men, and decided to wait until the morning, for the arrival of their supervisor, who would know what to do with their valuable find.

Two burly warriors squatted on their heels at the periphery of the circle, armed with their spears and shields. The bulk of the warriors curled on the ground, and one by one drifted to sleep. Rama and Herby leaned against each other and slept.

The forest around Jali settled into its nocturnal rhythm. He settled on a patch of narrow-leaved grass, feeling comforted by the familiar cricket-trills. Brelize nestled on his knee. Above his head, the fireflies dimmed,

and around him his troop of squirrels watched, until he
nodded off into his first slumber on planet Earth.

* * * * * *

CHAPTER FOUR

Majestic One

First morning

DAWN SPRINKLED HER soft sunrays over the dewy stirring forest. In the clearing, the warriors and prisoners continued to sleep, as Jali, Brelize and the troop of squirrels watched from under the cover of the trees.

A distant rumble alerted the guards, and they sprang tall before bellowing to the snoozing army. The warriors buzzed around, checked on the prisoners, and positioned themselves close by. The duo blinked rapidly, and all heads turned toward the approaching roll. From behind the forest dwelling, a long open truck trailed dust and screeched to a halt near the warriors.

A muscular dark man, similar to the warriors, leaped out of the vehicle, and he too wielded a spear and shield. The guards addressed him as Big Boss and hurried behind him to the prisoners.

Jali's ears tuned in.

Big Boss spoke, but the prisoners did not understand. Rama pointed to the forest, letting out muffled sounds through his gagged mouth. Big Boss shook his head from side to side, stomped around them, and returned to the truck. The warriors pushed Rama and Herby into the vehicle, and jumped in with their spears and shields. The vehicle sped past the dwelling and farther into the forest.

Jali and Brelize followed, darting through the woods as fast as their legs allowed. For thirty minutes, they tailed the prisoners, until the clatter slowed. Jali squinted while he sneaked around the bushes, pausing to catch his breath and wipe the sweat off his hot neck.

On an incline, the outline of a village, encircled by a barricade of closely knit wooden spikes, emerged. The truck entered the circle through a narrow opening, and stopped a few meters from a ring of dwellings. Big Boss rushed to an ornately thatched mud abode. Rama and Herby struggled as the warriors dragged them to a pile of thick logs.

Big Boss exited the abode, followed by a tall, formidable figure carrying an elaborate elongated spear and broad shield. His extravagant loin cloth and bracelets set him apart from the rest of the warriors. A long slender feather atop his headdress swayed in motion with his steps.

The warriors bowed. "Majestic One." They greeted him and stood to attention. He glared at Rama and Herby and ordered the guards to remove the gags.

"You Dragons dare to enter our tribal land?" he uttered in a loud voice, his large black eyes widened.

Jali's heart skipped a beat, and Brelize's tail twitched before she disappeared behind his legs.

This time Rama understood the language.

"We're not part of the Dragons. We oppose them."

But Majestic One grunted. "We have preserved our tradition, these tribal lands, our tribal villages and this umuzi for many centuries." He glared at Herby. "First you white men came and destroyed our people and land." He kicked him; the doctor keeled over in pain.

Majestic One's voice thickened with anger. "Then we got our freedom but only for a while, until all the rich, of every color, made slaves of the uneducated, fed off their fear, and got powerful."

He approached Rama with the spear raised high, and his eyes smoldered. "We thought we were the only ones suffering, until we learned the whole world's gone crazy, hating those different from the rich ones, hunting and killing anyone who threatens their power. That is the world you live in, out there!" He pointed past the forest. "Power is your new god!" In one quick motion he drove his spear deep into the ground as Rama spun, narrowly escaping.

Jali felt a chill settle deep in his bones.

Rama looked to the sky. "There's hope for your tribe and us. We want peace too. We can have it if we work together."

But Majestic One folded his arms and turned away.

"I'm one of the leaders of the First Ones, and our mission is to destroy the Dragons," Rama said.

"You're spies, like the hundreds who came before you. Still greedy after the technological meltdown fifty years ago. We know you seek to take over all we have worked hard to preserve!" Majestic One said.

He switched to his tribal language and motioned to the warriors. "String them on the stake, and let them die slowly. I'm sure our lammergeyer vulture-friends will have a feast of their bones." He wrenched his spear from the ground. The warriors bowed before he disappeared into the dwelling.

✳ ✳ ✳ ✳ ✳ ✳

CHAPTER FIVE

Umuzi Tribal Village

THE WARRIORS DRAGGED Rama and Herby and tied them to a wooden stake. They did not protest, and appeared to give in to their plight.

Jali could not stop shivering. I must do something. This is it, Reena and Commander ZW1. I must help them.

The small troop of squirrels tugged at his pants, and Brelize ran up his arm. Yes, his time had arrived. Hiding his pointed ears and Third Eye with the Earth-boy hood, he brazenly stepped out of the bush.

As he neared the bound and gagged duo, Herby noticed. He brushed Rama, and they shook their heads from side to side, their eyes wide. A barrage of sounds bombarded Jali's head.

"Don't come here, Prince! Run, hide, please," said

Herby's voice.

"Kid, stop, get out of here, NOW!" screamed Rama's voice.

Jali froze in his tracks. *I can hear their thoughts!*

Armed with confidence, he plodded on. One warrior turned. He pointed to Jali. The others followed suit and froze as they stared at the small hooded figure approaching them.

Big Boss raced to the dwelling, reappearing with Majestic One.

"Who comes forth?" Majestic One yelled.

Three guards formed a protective barrier around him.

In steady strides, Jali continued toward the prisoners.

"Stop!" Majestic One shouted. "Who are you?"

Jali's heart raced and he paused. "Esteemed leader of the tribal umuzi village, Majestic One." He bowed, his lower lip trembling. "I am here to negotiate with you over the plight of the two prisoners."

"You speak fluent Zulu with no accent!"

Jali continued to draw near.

"Stop!"

He paused, pursed his lower lip to hide the tremble, took in a deep breath, and waited.

"Lower your hood; show your face!"

"I come in peace, I am no threat to your tribal

village."

"Take off your hood, and show your face, child!"

He stiffened. *Oh no, now what do I do?*

Majestic One commanded the warriors and they ran toward Jali. His heart skipped a beat. He instinctively extended his right hand.

"Halt," he said, his voice high pitched.

The warriors stopped; confused they turned to Majestic One, who clicked his tongue, frustrated with their hesitance, and urged them to seize him.

There was no turning back. His breath deepened as he looked to the Cosmos. Somewhere up there Reena, Commander ZW1, and the Magnificent ZW7 watched from Zooble. He had to decide his next move.

In gradual movements, he dropped back the Earth-boy hood.

Loud gasps rippled from the warriors. They dropped to their knees and bowed their heads in a gesture of deep respect. Majestic One's spear fell. Annoyed, he motioned to his guard to get it. Spear in hand, he marched through the petrified crowd. Squinting in the light of the rising sun, he looked into Jali's face, stretched his strong neck back, and laughed. With tremendous force, he pierced the spear into the ground and shook his shield high above his head.

Jali trembled with fear.

"Get up, you morons!" he yelled at the immobilized warriors. "He's a child, with a strange costume! Get up!"

The warriors slowly raised their heads but kept their gazes lowered.

Majestic One walked around Jali. "How is it that you speak like us?"

He swallowed hard.

Majestic One turned, deep in thought, and chuckled. "Heh, heh, heh. I see. You have an African nanny in your big mansion." His headdress swayed. "Daddy and Mommy are too busy stealing dignity from our people." He pointed his long finger at Jali. "You learn our language from our African mama." He pounded his fist on his muscular chest. His eyes glinted, and his white teeth flashed, as he bellowed. "Tie him up! The vultures are going to love his tender bones."

The warriors straightened their legs but remained glued, their gazes fixed on Jali's feet where Brelize and the troop of red squirrels stood on hind legs.

"Come on, tie him up. You're wasting my time." Majestic One turned to Big Boss. "Check on that truck the Indi fella talked about; we can use it in our armament." But no one moved.

He commanded the three guards around him. "Tie him up now!"

The guards edged toward Jali.

His Third Eye fluttered; it scanned the village.

"Hayibo!" The guards clasped their heads and knelt. They bowed, as did each warrior.

"Are you crazy? Do I have to tie this child up myself? Give me the rope!" Majestic One snatched the rope from the quivering guard and rushed to Jali with it stretched between his hands, his large eyes pitch-black with fury.

Jali's heart skipped a beat. His ears perked.

A warmth rushed up his neck and His Third Eye opened wide.

Majestic One froze. He stepped back, turned, and dashed into a larger thatched mud dwelling at the side of the village.

Herby and Rama exchanged glances, their mouths agape, and stared at Jali.

His heart pounded. *My Third Eye is open!*

Majestic One nipped out, and back in. Not a sound was heard anywhere among the petrified men.

✳ ✳ ✳ ✳ ✳ ✳

CHAPTER SIX

Mystical Wise One

MAJESTIC ONE POPPED out of the thatched abode; he waited at the side of the entrance, his body stiff. His shoulders puffed out his muscular chest, and he clasped his spear and shield in a dignified stance.

A hum rang amid the warriors.

Jali sighed, long and deep.

Calmness descended.

His Third Eye fluttered and closed.

His ears perked.

An elder woman hobbled on a carved wooden stick, it's length streaked red and orange. Similar paintings splashed around her bare arms. Long white hair, a startling contrast to her ebony skin, flowed around her and swept to the ground. A decorative cloth draped her slender body. She was bare-footed, like the rest of the warriors.

She eyed the bowed men, fixed her gaze on Jali, and smiled.

He smiled and skipped to her.

Majestic One stepped in front of her. "Aikona, Wise One."

But she raised her stick and he stepped aside.

Jali bowed, lifted his head, and looked deep into her black eyes.

They both smiled.

"Rise!" she commanded the warriors. "And let the child be."

They unpeeled themselves from the ground, and hovered, mesmerized.

"Come walk with me, child," she said.

The umuzi village buzzed with chatter. Children of all ages, men, women, and elders appeared from their dwellings to witness the sight.

Jali and Wise One continued on a sandy patch to a expanse of smooth white rock under a wide tree. She placed her hand on his shoulder and lowered herself. The ornate stick stayed upright on the sand. Jali sat cross-legged on the ground in the shade in front of her. Wise One rested her hand on his head, looked to the skies, and smiled. The red and orange sand paintings on her arm and stick sparkled in the morning sunlight.

Warriors, families, and children gathered around them.

"Tell me how we can help you, little one?" she asked.

"Wise One, I—"

"No need for words, little one."

She reached for his cold hands, and kissed them with her soft lips. Placing them at her heart she closed her eyes.

Roses. The scent of roses filled his nostrils, and he felt himself floating in clouds of bliss. In the distance, Grandma slept in her Royal Bed on planet Zooka. Reena and Commander ZW1 watched planet Earth from Zooble intergalactic space explorer.

The grip on his hand tightened and he returned to the present to moment; Wise One frowned.

"We must hurry." She called Majestic One. "Son, untie the men."

He hesitated for a split second, then sprang into action. The warriors escorted the anxious looking Herby and Rama to her. On witnessing the hospitality surrounding Jali, their faces relaxed.

"Give them all the help to fix their truck; treat them as your brothers. They must leave before the sky darkens," Wise One instructed Majestic One, then turned to Jali. "Little one, come with me."

Like two finally reunited friends, they explored the village with Brelize and the squirrels. Animated children ran to them, and followed their trail. Along the circular path, warriors sharpened their spears, and elders rocked sleeping babies in hammocks.

At the outskirts of the umuzi circle, young women filled containers with water from the river, winding through the settlement. Under the spread of wide treetops, older men and women instructed groups of youngsters.

Wise One pointed to one session. "Come, let us join them, and see how these educators teach our little ones the history of our Zulu tribe, the country's tribes, the world's tribes, and our future together as peaceful beings."

Jali sighed. *I miss Guardian 1 and our lessons.*

Wise One read his thoughts. "We don't want you to lose out on your training." She smiled and motioned to him. "Come, let's find our special tribal Teacher, who resides away from our huts."

They made their way through a row of thatched huts, and neared a low fence swathed with blooming ferns. Wise One poked her stick to the far right and parted the fern flowers to reveal an ancient man with a toothless grin.

"The little one must polish his Third Eye skills," Wise One said.

The tribal Teacher smiled and bowed. "I've been

expecting you, Prince. Come." He gestured and led Jali through a hidden garden toward a solitary rock cave, decked with an assortment of purple and white butterflies. Banana and papaya trees laden with ripened fruit, and strelitzia bird plants with orange sepals and purple-white petals lined his path. What a delightful embracing scene.

If he did not know any better, he would have thought he was at his secret hideout on Zooka.

Behind him, Wise One called to Brelize and her troop of squirrels to follow her out of the garden.

❋ ❋ ❋ ❋ ❋ ❋

JALI ACCOMPANIED THE tribal Teacher into the cave and a myriad of chambers. Vertical shafts, deep passages, and brilliant azure pools welcomed him. *This is an exact replica of the Royal Training Cave!*

"Do you like it?" the Teacher asked. His eyes twinkled as he turned to the red lotus paintings on the far wall of the sloping chamber where they had stopped. "I want you feel at home."

Jali's Third Eye fluttered, and his ears perked. *That voice.*

"Excellent," the familiar voice replied as the figure turned toward him.

He gasped.

"I heard that you are eager to continue your royal training, Prince Jali."

He was staring at Guardian 1!

"Ready, Prince Jali?"

"Y-yes, Guardian 1," he stammered.

"Your last lesson on Zooka, terminated with you unable to sustain Third Eye visibility. Let us begin at step one: open Third Eye willfully."

Without a moment to lose, Jali composed himself and continued his Third Eye training in the middle of the tribal village, in the magical Draco mountain forest of KwaZulu-Natal in the heart of South Africa, on planet Earth.

I must graduate to Level-5.

He followed each guideline he had learned during the previous lesson with Guardian 1.

He stood tall, his arms relaxed at his sides, his gaze lowered. He took in a deep breath and focused.

He waited.

And waited.

And waited.

Nothing.

He tried again, taking in an even deeper breath, and focused.

Nothing.

He waited.

And waited.

And waited.

Try as he might, he failed once again to complete the first and most important step, to open his Third Eye at will.

He shuffled his feet and bit his lip. *I will be stuck in Level-4 forever! I will never be of any use to Zooka, Reena, and my dearest Grandma!*

The long white cape flowed around Guardian 1, as he walked back and forth with his hands locked behind him.

Jali sighed and he felt the sting of tears. *"Grandma."*

Guardian 1's Third Eye opened wide and stared directly at him. "Prince Jali, yes, Queen Vraka is weakened."

He could not help but blink fast, as hot tears bubbled and streamed down his face.

"Prince Jali, the longer you remain here, unprotected from negative forces, the weaker Grandma becomes."

The image of Grandma on the Royal Bed troubled him. *"What is wrong? How can I help Grandma?"*

"The sooner the Transporter extracts you to Zooble, the safer you will be, Prince Jali, and Queen Vraka will recover instantly."

"But we are delayed now, what if we are delayed even further?"

"I am here because of the worst-case scenario, Prince Jali."

Jali's heart fluttered. *"What then?"*

"For now, your best defense is to strengthen your own powers."

"My own powers?"

"You see, Prince Jali, the true secret to activating your superpowers is to develop self-confidence and self-esteem. Realize this, even if you wield powerful weapons, like the Sword of Khadga, the Magical Arrows of Power or even the mightiest Spear of V, you will not excel. If you surround yourself with the fearless Magnificent ZW7 warriors, their powers will always be external to you. Those powers will never be your own powers."

He listened attentively as Guardian 1 continued.

"When you develop your own inner strength, your own inner courage, and your own inner determination, you can rise strong and defeat the worst enemy possible."

"Worst enemy possible? Is that the Dragons that Rama fights against, Guardian 1?"

His teacher smiled and shook his head. "Your worst enemy is within you, Prince Jali."

"Inside me?"

"There are two forces within each being. Force One is positive, compassionate, creative, wise, and insightful; a visionary force. Force Two is negative, selfish, destructive, foolish, and ignorant; a short-sighted force. To access your own superpowers, you must activate Force One at all times. The problem is that in any life form, at any time, any of these Forces can rule."

"What if Force Two rules in all life forms?"

"Wise question, Prince Jali. The Cosmic Laws have a safety switch."

"Safety switch?"

"Yes, safety switch. Like a pendulum, it swings in selected life forms. When Force Two rules, Force One rises and quells Force Two. Balance is restored, and the Cosmos returns to its natural course. Understood, Prince Jali?"

"Yes! When I am self-confident and develop self-esteem, my Force One will be strong, I will not rely on Zooble, Princess Reena, Magnificent ZW7 warriors, or the extraction process to be visionary and insightful."

"Well said, Prince Jali."

"Will Grandma feel stronger?"

"Yes, Prince Jali, Queen Vraka will feel stronger when you are stronger. Understood?"

"Yes, Guardian 1, understood."

With renewed motivation, he parted his feet, rested his arms at his sides, and pushed his chest out, in Zookian royal warrior stance. He lowered his gaze, took in a deep breath, and focused. A surge of energy spiraled up his spine, spread through the back of his head, rose to the front of his forehead, and settled at his Third Eye.

His Third Eye fluttered and opened.

Bright white light bathed him.

He floated.

Below him was the training cave; outside the secret garden, children played in the sandy tribal village and Wise One smiled. He floated higher. Around him, the atmosphere sparkled crystal clear and Zooble hovered over planet Earth. Reena and Commander ZW1 waved from the Control Chamber. Beyond, far off in the Cosmos, on planet Zooka, Grandma lay in the Royal Bed, with Protector 1 at her side. She propped herself, beamed her enchanting smile, and waved.

His heart calmed and he smiled. Slowly he retracted his Third Eye vision. The light slowly dimmed. His Third Eye fluttered and closed.

He smiled at Guardian 1.

"Well done, Prince Jali," Guardian 1 said. "Remember, keep your Force One nourished and strong. Force Two will try to take over at any moment. Only you can tame your imposing Force, called the Impostor. Tame the Impostor within, Prince Jali, and you will shine bright always."

"I understand, Guardian 1. I must tame my Impostor."

❋ ❋ ❋ ❋ ❋ ❋

CHAPTER SEVEN

Tribal Dance of Africa

I BELIEVE WISE ONE is ready to feed you, Prince Jali. You can learn much from her Tribal Cane." Guardian 1 said.

Wise One shuffled into the entrance of the stony chamber, with Brelize and her squirrels hopping at her feet.

"Come, little one, our people have prepared your favorite meal," she said.

Jali turned to thank Guardian 1, and found the tribal Teacher grinning instead! The elder bowed, and winked.

"Thank you, tribal Teacher, for taking such good care of our little one," Wise One said, with a hint of mischief in her voice.

They bid him farewell and strolled through the exotic

garden, exited the fern fence, and were once more in the tribal village. Wise One guided to Jali to the white stone bedecked with spotted yellow mangoes, a pile of white African macadamia nuts, and spread of cacao cake.

The Zulu children joined them, and chomp by chomp they devoured every morsel off the stone.

"Our children have something to show you, little one," Wise One said.

A group of youngsters rallied in front of him, bumping against each other, giggling, their musical ankle bracelets chiming. The girls, in blue beaded grass skirts, and the boys in loin cloths, formed a circle. Five drummers sat behind them, beating sticks on clay pot drums, while the villagers bustled to watch.

The children jumped and twisted in the air, landing low. Their arms swung back and forth, and they swiveled in rhythm with the intoxicating drumming and shrill guttural chanting from young women. A little girl, gyrating her hips, called to Jali. Laughter and delight echoed as he danced the ancient tribal dance in tempo with the young dancers.

Around them, the glorious Draco mountain ignited rich red in the afternoon sunshine. Branches dipped in cadence. Bald headed eagles swooped and rose over the dancers, and Brelize and the squirrels pirouetted with joy. Wise One swayed, and the red sand paintings on her arms and her Tribal Cane twirled around her flowing long white hair.

Slowly, the drumbeats subsided, and the children scattered.

"You dance like an African," Wise One said. She laughed. "You know, an African is not one born in Africa but is one who cares about the future of the people. So, you are an African."

The energetic bopping and afternoon sunshine warmed him. Beads of sweat tickled his face, and he sought respite at Wise One's feet under the gigantic tree.

"This is our ancient uSolu tree, Prince Jali, favorite of our revered elephants and ethalion butterflies, and a place where our tribe gathers in the summer, for protective shade."

He stretched his neck. Yes he could see why. Wedges of reddish-brown bark wound up the forty-meter tree, and its flat crown of leaves spread wide.

"Little one, you have an important role before you return to Zooka."

His ears perked. *Me, an important role?*

"The First One, Kriaka Adi, will lead you to the Portal at Mont Aux Sources. She has hidden her powers inside the GIFT, the precious White Stone that the Dragons and the whole planet now seek. She is in grave danger. To save her, you will be forced to make a sacrifice.

You will know when the time is right."

"I *will* help Kriaka Adi, Wise One. I promise."

"I know. I know you are determined to do so. Little one, you must look inside you. Your legacy is one of peace and unity. The Impostor will possess many around you. It will lead you astray many a time. But you must remember Force One. Remember your legacy. Your mama and papa lived and gave their lives for the peace for which you strive."

He watched her with great intent.

"Find the one to fly with, and strengthen yourself on this planet. Be wary of the disguised ones, for they plot against you."

A string of questions ran through his mind, but a frolicking crowd in the distance interrupted them. Children giggled as they ran to the approaching Rama, Herby, and Majestic One. The trio smiled.

Majestic One bowed and reported on their progress. "The truck they call Jen is fixed and loaded with food packs. I installed our undetectable route plotter in their vehicle."

Wise One reached to Jali. "Little one, take this amulet." She draped a knitted grass rope over his neck and adjusted a tiny emerald amulet on his chest. "It will keep your temperature regulated on our planet."

She winked, and the village elders, women, men,

children, and warriors flocked around the group ready to depart.

"Farewell, little one. Say 'Vitte lukka' to Grandma back on Zooka."

He hugged her and bowed to Majestic One. He looked around, but there was no sign of the tribal Teacher.

Jali, Herby and Rama joined Majestic One, who escorted them to the repaired truck. "We are part of your team now. We will prepare the villages around the provinces, and spread the word throughout our African continent and further, to ready the pure beings for the ordained time. We'll prepare to meet you at Mont Aux Sources," he said.

Ahead of them, Jen awaited, amid cheers and bows from the tribal village.

"Prince Jali, I'm so proud of you. We both are," Herby said, pulling him close.

Rama nodded and ruffled his hair. "You saved us, Prince Jali."

The praises from the men boosted his confidence as he settled into his familiar spot in the truck. He smiled with joy when Rama started Jen. All around them, the villagers danced and waved goodbye.

Within minutes of leaving the gates of the umuzi village, unable to with hold the information imparted to him, he leaned forward and whispered. "We must save

Kriaka Adi."

"What?" Herby and Rama said in unison.

"The Wise One. She said that Kriaka Adi may be in danger."

Rama's face reddened. "We have the best back route to Sherman's Cave. We'll get there by nightfall."

He revved Jen and they sped through the forest.

✳ ✳ ✳ ✳ ✳ ✳

CHAPTER EIGHT

Kidnapped

JEN FORGED THROUGH the rugged mountain path flanked by towering rocky ranges, her occupants absorbed in their thoughts. Jali, already acclimatized to the rough ride, bounced about with Brelize. He reconstructed his adventurous day in the umuzi village. Every word and every image dangled fresh in his memory.

The one that flies. Of course, that is Tuttles. But he is on Zooble!

Nothing made sense. He reminisced about the astounding and unexpected training session with Guardian 1 and smiled. His newly acquired willful superpowers could serve him well on this planet.

In the front seats, the men remained entrenched in their thoughts, oblivious to their surroundings. This was the perfect opportunity for him to use his visionary powers to locate Tuttles.

He closed his eyes, inhaled deeply and focused on his Third Eye.

He waited.

And waited.

And waited.

In vain.

He frowned. *What is wrong? Why can I not use my superpowers at my beckoning?*

Brelize rose on her hind paws and echoed his sentiments.

He shrugged. It was futile.

She resumed her favorite position in his Earth-boy hood, and pointed to the scenery that flashed past them.

The crisp mountain air caressed his face, and he relished the array of recognizable flowery scents. Today could have been just one more moment in his fourteen Z-years of existence on Zooka.

But here he was.

For the first time since leaving home, he realized that he had survived a complete day on planet Earth. He was truly living his dream of intergalactic adventures.

❋ ❋ ❋ ❋ ❋ ❋

THE HOLLOW IN the pit of Herby's stomach worsened. Three hours passed while Jen zipped through the hidden trails in the valley of Monk's Cowl, guided by Majestic One's hand-made route plotter. Thankfully, they remained undetected through the mountain passes and the Cathedral forest.

Up ahead the rotting signpost for Cathedral Peak appeared. At any minute, they would arrive at the trail head to Sherman's Cave. There it was!

His heart raced. In front of them, Pierre's sports car jutted from the partially concealed trail at the foot of an incline.

He pointed with excitement. "They're here."

"That's a good sign!" Rama shouted and screeched to a halt.

He leaped out before Rama and peered inside the deserted vehicle. An anxious smile quivered on his lips. "They must be in the cave."

Rama strapped food packs over his back, while he grabbed the medical bag and sleeping gear. He strained his neck and tried to view past the compact treetops.

"Okay, time to scramble up," Rama said, parting the bushes and leading the way.

He adjusted the prince's hood and followed close behind him, anxious to reach the top. The pending sunset revitalized the mountain sky with its final burst of fiery orange, and the threesome hiked in haste.

The time seemed to stretch and stretch and stretch, and he struggled to maintain his patience, eager to see Kri again.

Ahead of them, Rama slowed and pointed. "Look, there's the cave."

Unable to wait any longer, he rushed past the prince and bumped into Rama. They ran along the wide bushy plateau to the low overhang of the cave entrance.

"Kri, Shiana, Siya?" Rama shouted.

Shiana bolted from the cave and jumped into his arms. "What's the matter?" Rama asked.

Siya sided out, his face somber.

Herby pleaded to the boy. "Kri?"

The boy shuffled, his head hung low. He tugged at his long braids.

Herby, on the brink of hysteria, repeated. "Where is Kri?"

A shadow filled the opening of the cave.

"Kri?" He screamed and bolted toward the figure.

But that man, Pierre stepped into the light.

"Where's Kri?" he shouted, and darted his gaze around the shallow empty cave.

At his side, Rama, his chest heaving, spat out at Pierre, "Where's my sister, Pierre?"

Pierre ran his hand across his face, and shook his head. "They got her, man!"

Herby, unable to contain his fury any longer, lunged at the man, ramming him against the stone wall. He beat at him until Rama hauled him off and shoved him away.

His face felt hot, and for the first time in his life he could not cap his rage. "I told you we couldn't trust him!" he shouted at Rama, his heart racing. "What happened Pierre? Why did you let this happen?" he yelled, and in a flash jumped at the man once more, and punched hard.

Rama yanked him off and restrained him against the side of the cave, glaring at him and silencing him with his finger. With enormous reluctance, he rooted his feet to the ground, as Rama turned to Pierre.

The man steadied himself and stretched his jaw. "We stopped in Winterton, for a toilet break. The kids were peeing. Before I knew what was happening, the Dragons... the Dragons, man... they came from nowhere. Michael, Chan's son, was shouting and they knocked me out. When I came to, the kids were there and Kriaka was gone."

The cave blurred; Herby blinked fast to clear his vision, trying to understand.

"A-Aka's gone!" Shiana cried, and ran to Rama. He let go of Herby and embraced her distraught little figure.

The men glared at Pierre wiping blood off his chin. "I remembered what Kriaka told me about this place, and we raced here."

Shiana rocked herself hysterically. Rama knelt in front of her and spoke in soft tones. "Is that what happened, Shiana?"

"Yeah, I w-w-wanted to p-p-pee," she stammered. "Siya waited at the t-toilet door. There was a strange s-sound. When we got t-to the car, the doors were open and Pierre was on the ground. There was b-b-blood in the back."

"Blood!" Herby's heart lurched. He lunged for Pierre, but Rama jumped and held him back.

Pierre interrupted. "That loud cat, she was squealing like crazy. I think they snapped her neck and threw her away. I didn't want to risk searching for her, so we headed here."

"They killed M-Meosic," Shiana cried, sobbing, and beside her Siya nodded, his face wet.

Herby rushed for Pierre and knocked him down. "You dirty scoundrel, I should never have trusted you with my Kri." He landed punch after punch on the man's face, and could not understand why Rama once again came to culprit's rescue, and pushed back hard on his tense body.

Pierre dabbed his nose and muttered. "I heard Michael talk about where they're taking her tomorrow. I think I know where it is." He darted a look at the men and raised himself.

"Tomorrow?" Herby said.

"Yeah, something about hiding her for two nights, then moving her for interrogation."

They're going to interrogate my Angel! He groaned and his stomach tightened. His feet prepared for another strike.

"Go cool off, Herby!" Rama shouted. He called to the prince. "Go with him, kid."

Against his will, he let the boy guide him to the low opening. Behind them Rama teamed up with Pierre. "Come on, we've got to figure out where they're planning to take Kri. We must find her tomorrow." He pulled a map from his duffle bag and spread it on the floor of the cave.

Herby glared back at Pierre. "This should never have happened," he said.

A tug at his hand distracted him. Shiana cried. "W-w-we must find Aka." She squeezed herself against him. He cradled her hot head, knelt, and wiped away her tears. He motioned to Siya to check the bag of food and water and stay with her.

"Let's walk, Prince."

The cool afternoon breeze soothed his flushed face, but his pulse was still on the run.

Maybe the prince can help locate Kri.

As soon as they were out of earshot, he asked, "Prince, can you see or hear Kri?"

The boy shook his head and bit his lip. "Doctor Herby, I can only see imminent danger to me. Wise One said Kriaka Adi was in danger. That is all I know."

He scrunched his lips. *Oh no.*

The prince turned to him. "Why are the Dragons after Kriaka Adi when she is kind and gentle and incapable of hurting anyone?"

He sighed heavily, and steered the little figure toward the flow of the creek. Fireflies hovered over the boy's hooded head, and the little rusty-red squirrel tugged at his ankles and ran up to his shoulder.

"There you are, Brelize," the prince said. "Siya and Shiana have some nuts for you."

The little creature squeaked, stuck out her tongue, and ran to the duo.

His heart skipped a beat. "You talk to the animals as if they understand you, Prince Jali."

"We can understand each other," the boy said.

He squeezed his eyebrows and stifled a sob. "That's so beautiful, so beautiful."

He swallowed hard, and a picture of Kri flashed before him. "I adored Kri from the day I saw her talking to the animals. She was just fifteen." His eyes welled, but he smiled at the memory of her. "We were not far from here on a hiking trail in the Champagne Valley... with our parents. They were bosom buddies, you know." He sniffed. "Kri ignored me, why not, I was a clumsy nerd.

"She kept talking to the little plants and snails. I

asked her why she did that. She said, 'We're all the same beings, just in different forms.' I thought that was funny, so I debated that humans were superior to the animals and trees, that we could speak and think. 'No,' she said, and placed a little rough rain frog in my palm."

He opened his palm; the sensation of it's webbed feet lingered as if it was yesterday.

"Then she said, 'Little being, show my friend that he is wrong, come over to me now.' And that frog jumped from my hand to hers. I fell in love with her from that moment on, but she never guessed." He bent, picked a piece of litter off the trail, and stuck it in his pocket.

After a deep sigh, he continued. "We humans have made a mess of our planet. All my Kri wants is to bring hope to those who are kind and compassionate and treat all equally."

"Doctor Herby, are peace and equality threats to the Opposition, the Force Two?"

"Force Two?"

"Yes, my Guardian 1 says that when the negative force within us dominates, we turn into our own worst enemy, the Impostor."

It made sense. He wrinkled his eyebrows and nodded. "Ja, when the Dragons killed our parents in front of Rama, Kri rushed home from the US. She was twenty-five. Come to think of it, from then the Dragons got worse.

They seemed afraid of her."

"Doctor Herby, could their fear be related to the GIFT?"

He pondered for a moment; the prince had a point. "Ja, ja, Kri's mother had always carried a little white stone in her bag, and when she died Kri found it hidden in the rose garden. She was devastated by the death of her parents and locked herself in their room for three whole days. Rama and I checked through the window each day. We eventually stormed the room."

His pulse raced at the vivid memory. "Kri sat on the floor—her vitals were normal, but she seemed to be in a deep sleep." The image of her slender figure in the trance-like state flashed through his mind. "I stayed with her for another two days, making sure she was good. Then she got up, showed me the stone, and said we must save the pure ones. She's kept the stone with her ever since. Believe it or not, over the past ten years that stone glowed on her birthdays."

The prince leaned forward and spoke in a soft tone. "Did anyone notice?"

He shook his head, but somehow the prince's words cast a web of doubts. "She kept the stone secretly stowed away from prying eyes. But people became attracted to her energy, and they started to gather with her for meditation sessions. Only Rama and I knew about the

Dikóná

stone, or so I thought until now. We figured she'd go back
to Chicago, but she never mentioned it. I knew for a long
time that she'd be my only love."

The African night sky glittered; the Orion Nebula
clearly visible. He pointed. "See there, Prince, there is our
special constellation, Columba the Dove, the bearer of
peace."

The prince looked closely, his head following his
finger.

"See, it's close to the faithful dog, Canis Major, and
Lepus the Hare. Columba is the place Kri and I escape to
in our dreams each night, where everyone is kind and
happy." He sighed and they stared into the star-speckled
sky.

A rustle behind them revealed Siya and Shiana. "W-
w-we're gonna find Aka? P-p-promise?" She wrapped
her tiny body against him.

He kissed her head. Feeling fully determined to
rescue Kri, he made his way back to the cave. "I'm gonna
go help them to find our Kri." He turned to the youngsters
and whispered. "Don't worry, I'll keep a close eye on that
Pierre."

❋ ❋ ❋ ❋ ❋ ❋

CHAPTER NINE

Visionary Utopian Glass

JALI REMAINED MESMERIZED with the constellations, a red planet and four moons, and he mused on the doctor's utopian spot in the Cosmos.

He made way for Siya, who plonked himself on the boulder beside him and followed his gaze. "Do *you* come from there, Prince?"

He grinned. "No, much farther, Siya, much farther."

The boy gasped. "Farther than the Princess constellation and the Andromeda galaxy?"

"Princess?" Jali said, and he chuckled. "Yes, much farther than her and the galaxy."

The boy stared at him and frowned. "Prince, what happened? We waited for you last night. We were worried. I thought the Dragons got you too!" His gaze fixed on Jali's amulet. "What's the grass rope and stone,

Prince?"

He smiled. "Wise One in the tribal village gave it to me."

"Hayibo, you went into the tribal village!"

Shiana shuffled close. Ignoring the boy's chatter, she held Jali's hand. "Will you h-h-help us find Aka?" Her big eyes teared. "W-w-won't Princess Reena know what to do?"

His heart skipped a beat, and he sighed. Yes Reena could help. He quickly scanned their location, leaned close, and whispered, "Let's go around the back of the cave."

The trio, followed by Brelize, hurried. A cloistered spot, between the shrubs, was perfectly hidden by tall trees. On his instructions, his furry friend stayed on guard.

With his eyes closed, he took in a deep breath, and let it out. His Third Eye fluttered, but did not open. He tried to focus once more. His Third Eye opened but shut again. *Oh no, not again!*

Next to him, Shiana's blue tearful eyes stared at him, pleading. He could not fail her. Shutting his eyes, he remembered Guardian 1's words: *tame the Impostor.*

With all the energy he could muster, he focused. His breathing deepened, and a stillness swept through him. His Third Eye opened at his instruction. The atmosphere around him crackled and filled with blue light.

"Reena?" he said in hushed tones.

Reena and Commander ZW1 appeared in the Zookian Glass. "Prince Jali, we can observe you, but we are unable to effect direct contact with you. Only you can make contact. Tread with caution. Be wary, for each time you initiate contact you become more Earth-like and lose your Third Eye powers," Commander ZW1 said.

Jali shuffled nervously and stared at his sister. "How can I prevent losing my powers, Reena?"

"You would need to recharge your energies to regain Zookian Third Eye powers. We are uncertain of how you can do so within the planet's perplexing and unstable vibrations."

His palms felt damp; he could not wait any longer. "Reena, how is Grandma?"

"Grandma remains weak. Her low energy is linked to your presence on Earth."

His heart pounded, and he took in a sharp breath.

"Jee, you must find Kriaka Adi, for she is the key to you opening the Portal."

"Reena, Wise One said to tell Grandma 'Vitte Lukka.'"

"Yes, already transmitted," Reena acknowledged. "Remember, Jee, we can see all that you see, and hear all that you hear, and more. Most important, do not lose the

Thermo Regulator Amulet gifted to you."

He twirled the grass chain and plodded on with the reason for his contact. "I need Tuttles, Reena; can you send him to me?"

Reena and Commander ZW1 exchanged thoughts. "He is not here, Jee. He disappeared when you beamed onto planet Earth."

His heart lurched and his breath quickened.

"Listen, Jee, time is short, the transmission is terminating... Take care, brother..." The Zookian Glass faded.

His limbs trembled and folded, as he fell into Siya's arms.

"Rest a bit, Prince, your energy, it must come back," the boy said and rocked his exhausted body.

"Where is Tuttles? I must find him," he whispered.

Shiana clasped his hand. "P-P-Prince, I'll help."

She stretched her body flat on the ground. Her long golden tresses covered her face, and she whispered. "Help Prince Jali find Tuttles."

"What are you doing?" Siya asked.

"I'm asking the black giant ants to help find T-T-Tuttles!"

Jali smiled. Renewed energy flowed through him; he leaned against Siya and stood.

Just as the trio prepared to return to the cave, Brelize

waved her paws to alert them.

Herby's voice rang out, "Come in, kids."

Jali fit his Earth-boy hood snug over his head, before they emerged from the bushes to enter the cave.

❇ ❇ ❇ ❇ ❇ ❇

CHAPTER TEN

Love Pains

Second morning

HERBY HIKED CAREFULLY down the damp trail, followed by Shiana, Jali, Siya, Pierre, and Rama. The woody aroma from the early morning rain, reminded Jali of home. Droplets of water splattered on his nose, and he savored the pure taste of the planet's mountain rain. *Not any different from Zooka.*

Brelize hopped alongside him, leaping effortlessly over the sharp rocks and glistening pebbles. By the time they arrived at the vehicles still hidden at the foot of the trail, the mist cleared.

Rama propped the map on Jen's dashboard and gave instructions for their journey. "You drive ahead, Pierre, we'll follow."

The man agreed. "The boys can keep me company.

Come on, fellas."

Herby's head jutted out of the truck, and with an apparent look of concern he peered at Rama, who squinted and hesitated. "Huh, okay then."

Pierre motioned to the boys in a tone of excitement. "All right! Who wants to sit in the front?" He raised his eyebrows toward Jali's hooded head.

He froze.

Siya rushed to his rescue, taking up the man's offer. Relieved, Jali held onto his Earth-boy hood and squeezed through the tight space into the backseat. Within minutes of settling in, they set off on their mysterious mission, with Jen following close behind the sports car.

The plush interior was a stark contrast to Rama's self-constructed bakkie. He wriggled from a recognizable sensation under his hand. An animal's skin lined the seat! Perhaps his imagination played tricks on his mind? But Brelize popping out of his jacket pocket, assured him that he was indeed sitting on a dead animal's skin.

Unable to squirm any farther, he settled into the surprisingly gentle ride and scanned his new surroundings. *What are these buttons for?* He pressed on one to his right and reeled as the window opened.

Pierre poked his head in the back, startling him. He quickly adjusted his hood and pressed his back as far as he could into the seat.

The man's gaze fixated on the amulet, before returning his attention to road. "What's the neck chain about, little fella?"

Siya interrupted. "Nothing special."

Pierre grunted, and his voice piqued with curiosity. "You guys were late coming in yesterday; were you okay?" He glanced at Jali.

"They went through the tribal village." Siya said.

"Really!"

To Jali's delight, Rama honked and overtook them, interrupting the line of questions.

"Seems like good ol' Rama wants to lead for now," Pierre said, and chuckled.

Dust rose behind Jen, and grits of sand struck their vehicle. Pierre swerved. "I hate these mountain dirt roads; nothing like a good stretch of clean highway."

"You must live in a big house," Siya said.

Pierre's face darkened and he grunted. "Yeah, once upon a time, yeah, a big house, loads of servants, that was all before our world changed, yeah! Poof, no phones, no Internet, nothin'. Crikey, that sucked! Well, at least you fellas have nothing to miss. All before your time. Now here we are, trying to get back what was ours."

"I hope we can rescue Kriaka," Siya said.

The man remained silent for a few minutes. "Yeah, that Michael, Chan's son, he's quite a rascal. Brat. He thinks he's as powerful as his father. But he walks only in his shadow."

Pierre poked to the back and surprised Jali again. "Say, what's your name anyway?"

"Jali, he's my friend Jali," Siya said.

Pierre snorted. "Well, Jali, does your father smack you around?"

Even though he pressed himself back into the seat, as far away from the interrogation as he could get, it was inadequate.

He blinked rapidly to stop the tears. "My father passed on!"

"Oh, sorry, old chap."

"What about your mom? She slap you around?"

"She passed on too."

"Crikey. That stinks."

"What about your folks, Siya?" Pierre asked.

"They're gone too," Siya whispered.

Pierre glared at Siya and Jali. "And me? What about me?" The man prompted, in a thunderous voice.

The boys did not respond.

"Well, I'll tell you orphans my story. Parents, hmmm. My father treated me like dirt. I didn't look like him — too ugly, he said. He'd beat me whenever he could. My mom tried to protect me, but she loved him too much. More than me."

"Where are they now?" Siya whispered.

"Ah, all dead, no more…"

"Do you have children?" Siya asked.

Pierre chuckled; he snorted and slammed his hand onto the steering wheel. Jali's heart skipped a beat and Siya startled.

The man's knuckles whitened. "I once had a family, my beautiful delightful love. Sooo beautiful. Same story. One day the bad ones came and took away my Delight, my love. Poof! She was gone. *Gone!*" He slammed his hand on the wheel.

Jali swallowed hard; goose bumps formed on his ears.

"I locked myself away, in my work." The man rattled his fingers on the wheel. "Yeah, I'm rich, I can travel wherever I want, I can eat whatever I want, I can do whatever I want, but they tore something from me. They took my soul!"

In the deathly silence, the boys remained motionless, and Brelize clutched Jali's hand.

"I see her face wherever I go. I cannot rest until I wipe them out forever!"

Pierre's white knuckles clenched over the steering wheel.

They drove in absolute silence.

Deadened silence.

Somber silence.

Endless silence.

"What do you know!" Pierre shouted.

Jali, Brelize, and Siya gasped.

"We're a load of suckers in this car. Carrying heavy baggage!" He turned to Jali. "Us men, we have to be strong, yeah. It's up to us to set things right. You kids can join me in my happy place, if you want." He flashed his white teeth and his eyes glistened.

"Ay, Rama is stopping," Siya said.

They halted behind Jen.

Rama jumped out and waved. "Shiana needs to pee."

Relieved to escape the tension, Jali followed Siya and guarded Shiana at the nearby bushes. They turned away to give her privacy. When she finished, she ran to the opposite shrubs, quickly bent, and rushed to Jali. Her palm was filled with black ants. "I t-t-told them to spread the word about Tuttles."

"Shiana, come on, child." Rama beckoned to them. "We've just about two hours to go," he said. "Am I glad those Dragons aren't following us!"

"Ja, these back roads help," Herby replied.

They returned to the vehicles, and Pierre led the way on their last stretch to the destination.

Two hours passed in silence, as they continued through thickly wooded back roads, easterly, away from the safety of the Draco mountains.

The car slowed, and in the distance, the outline of a dwelling emerged. Jali turned and watched as Herby pointed, and the two men looked intently through Jen's dusty windshield.

Pierre swung the car to the left and drove into the bush. "This is as close as we need to go," he said, and pushed his way out. Jen parked close behind them, well hidden from the narrow, wooded dirt road.

Everyone got out and monitored the area.

"Hayibo, that's a castle!" Siya pointed to a massive dwelling rising high into the sky.

❋ ❋ ❋ ❋ ❋ ❋

CHAPTER ELEVEN

Mystery Castle

RAMA'S HEART RACED. He heaved the long black bag out of the truck, and without a word the men armed themselves. Behind them, the kids looked wide-eyed at the stack of armaments at the side of the truck.

Rama patted Shiana's head. "You kids stay here. Lock yourself in the truck."

Herby agreed, and followed Pierre through the bushes. Rama turned once more to wave to the children, before adjusting his cap, and rushing into the thick forest. They carefully made their way through the tall undergrowth, in the direction of the building. His heart pounded; thankfully the late afternoon sun cast a shadow in their favor. They trudged undetected all the way to a tall fence. Sweat streamed down his back, and his long hair clung to the back of his neck.

The castle towered above the barbed wire fence. Pierre bent low and motioned ahead, and they ran along its cover of bushes.

"We split up to take the front, back, and side entrances," Pierre whispered.

They agreed. An eerie silence filled the unkempt grounds, inhabited by a forest of trees. On the mossy brick castle walls, creeper ferns hung like dilapidated ladders. Herby and Pierre split and disappeared to the back and side. Rama stuck close to the barely discernible red bricks and crept toward the front entrance.

Columns of heavy wrought-iron barricades shielded the long row of lofty baroque windows from the outside world.

Not a Dragon was in sight.

The scene too quiet for comfort.

But the silence continued.

Deathly silence.

Until shots exploded.

Rama crouched, and his hair stood on end. *Kri!* He dashed to an immense carved wooden door.

He startled when Pierre popped from the side of the castle. "The back, the back!" the man shouted and pointed.

They ran down a stone path and reached the back entrance, and barged in through the open door. Rama's heart skipped a beat and he felt the sweat stream down his back. On the floor in front of him, Herby lay in a pool of blood. He checked his pulse while Pierre continued inside. *Yes, a pulse.*

He raced ahead and almost collided with Pierre. On the tiled floor of a vestibule, they found the motionless body of Michael, with a gun by his side.

Pierre ran ahead, but Rama stopped.

He slapped Michael's face. The young man stirred.

"Where is Kri?" Rama shouted.

"I don't know, I—" Michael whispered.

Pierre dashed back. "It's empty, there's no one here, man!"

Rama pulled the man off the floor, gripped his neck and shoved him against the wall.

"What do you mean you don't know?"

The young man shook his head, his blue eyes widened.

Rama jawed him. "You creep, you and the Dragons kidnapped Kri. You shot Herby." The man fell, and he shook him hard. "Where is she? Where is she, you rat?"

Michael blocked the blows. "Hey, I don't know what you're talking about, honest, I don't."

He punched him in the stomach, and the man screamed. "I didn't do it, I swear, this is my hideout, man!"

He pinned him against the wall, unable to accept his explanations. "I'm gonna kill you unless you tell me."

But Michael persisted with his denial, until Rama immobilized him, and cocked his gun to his head. The young man screamed and raised his hands above his head.

"Look, if the Dragons kidnapped her, I think I know where they took her."

"Kill him," Pierre shouted. "He's lying, kill him now."

A shuffling behind them caught Rama's attention. Herby! He staggered in and dropped to the floor. Rama ran to his side, and glared back at Michael. "You're comin' with us," he said. He lifted Herby off the floor and draped his arm around his neck.

Pierre kicked Michael and pushed him ahead. They lumbered through the garden, into the bushes, and back to the vehicles as fast as they could. The children ran to them, wide eyed.

Herby groaned. "My medical kit."

Siya and the prince ran ahead to the truck. Shiana held on to Herby's hand and sobbed.

"What's wrong, Herby? What's wrong? P-p-please don't die." She looked at Rama. "Where's Aka?"

He shook his head, lowered Herby into the back seat, and wrenched open the medical kit.

Blood oozed out of Herby's right side. He whispered, "Rama, we must find Kri before it's too late. I'll be okay."

Filled with fury, Rama lunged at Michael and squeezed his throat. "You better take us to Kri, *now*!" He raised his gun and shouted. "Or I swear I'll kill you right here."

"Yes, yes, I'll take you there," Michael replied. His bloodied face swelled with bruises.

Rama motioned to Pierre. "Take him with you. You lead. Siya can ride with you."

Pierre sped ahead, Rama following close, his face hot as he darted a look at Herby, stretched on the back seat, with the prince at his side. *Kri better be alive!*

✳ ✳ ✳ ✳ ✳ ✳

CHAPTER TWELVE

Chamber of Horrors

JALI'S BREATHING QUICKENED; and his Third Eye fluttered. Brelize clung in the safety of his Earth-boy hood. Beside them, Herby's blood-soaked lower body sprawled on the seat. Shiana leaned from the front, tears streaming down her face.

Herby stirred and spoke in a gruff voice. "Prince, I need your help."

He nodded.

"You must help find Kri."

Shiana cried. "P-P-Prince won't let anything bad happen to you, or to Kri."

The doctor coughed and pulled him close. "Prince, listen. Kri must be protected. She holds the key."

"Yes, I know, Doctor Herby. Reena told me Kriaka Adi is the only one who can open the Portal at Mont Aux

Sources."

Herby struggled to move his head and squeezed his eyes shut. "That's only part of it, Prince." He pulled him closer still. "Kri has special powers. It's all locked in the GIFT. I know now that is why the Dragons stole the GIFT—they want the power for themselves. But they need Kri; she is the key to using the GIFT. They can't use the GIFT without Kri, don't forget, they can't use the GIFT without Kri."

In a weak voice Herby added, "Keep an eye on Pierre, Prince."

Jali's heart raced, and hot tears rolled down his face. "I promise, Doctor Herby."

Herby choked. "You are a great prince." He squeezed his hand. "Now you must help me to remove the bullet in my side."

His Third Eye fluttered, and he felt faint. "Take out the bullet?"

"Yes, you are the only one who can do it. Will you help me, Prince? If we don't get it out now, that's it."

Jali swallowed hard; could he do it?

Herby ripped open his bloodied shirt. A wave of nausea rose in Jali. His Third Eye fluttered, and he quickly stabilized. The doctor poured a strong-smelling liquid over his skin. He held something sharp and metallic over the wound and pushed it in and groaned.

Shiana screamed and Brelize rattled. His heart pounded hard against his ribs.

The doctor moaned and he whispered, "The bullet is close to the surface, just use this and pull it out."

Jali threaded his fingers through the handles of the shiny instrument, gripping it tight in an effort to calm his trembling hand. Closing his eyes, he took a deep breath. A rush of energy shot up his spine, and his Third Eye opened. Confident, he placed his steady hand over Herby's wound, and with a short insertion, he wrenched out the bullet, and caught his breath.

"Good job, Prince." Herby wiped a strong-smelling cloth over the wound. "Help tie me up. I'll heal better. Don't worry, Shiana, all's well now." He handed Jali a roll of cloth.

He swiftly wrapped the wide muslin tight around Herby's body. He could feel the pounding of the doctor's heart.

"You did it, Prince!" Shiana shrieked from the front.

Rama darted a look back. He wiped his face and nodded.

Herby slumped and rested his damp head on Jali's lap. Jali sighed and sobbed silently, his arm around the doctor's face. He rocked him, and felt a sting of tears stream down his Zookian nose.

Brelize nestled in his Earth-boy hood and they drove

in a long, drawn-out silence.

✳ ✳ ✳ ✳ ✳ ✳

THEY HAD BEEN driving for over an hour when the truck swerved. Jali steadied himself and the doctor as Jen turned and drove down a long narrow bumpy path, shrouded by bushes.

When they could go no farther, Rama slowed to a halt and leaped out to join Michael and Pierre, peering past a high bush fence around a grassy incline. At the top of the hill, rose an enormous castle that miniaturized the one they had come from.

Jali's ears perked and he tuned into the men's discussions.

Michael whispered, "This is the place, I know it. I've been watching him for years. This is the Dragons' headquarters; it's an underground system of tunnels built hundreds of years ago."

Pierre shook his head at Rama. "This is a trap, man. There's an electric fence. Look, there are Dragon snipers around the roof and steeple, and there's a helicopter up there!"

Rama cussed. "Shoot, what the heck is this place?"

"This is the Dragons' top secret network of cutting-edge research for world domination, headed by my father."

"It's a fortress!" Rama said, as they checked over the

hedge.

"There's a hidden trapdoor on the left side. That's how we get in undetected," the young man reassured them.

"It's a trap," Pierre insisted, glaring at Michael.

Rama brushed him aside. "We've gotta get Kri out *now!*" He returned to the truck. "Kids, stay here with Herb—"

But while they were contemplating their next move, the doctor had insisted on Jali helping him out of the truck.

Herby shuffled. "No way, I must get Kri." He hopped over to the men.

"Okay, there's no time to waste, let's get going," Pierre said.

Jali watched as the men replenished their weapons and followed Michael. They ducked along the fence and stopped a short distance ahead to crawl under a concealed opening and up through the short grass to the left side of the hill. Michael pointed to a patch of dried grass and began digging through to the sand. Rama joined him. They dug fast and hard until they hit on a solid spot. Both men tugged at an exposed metal hook. It gave way, and under the cover of the bushes, they opened the trapdoor. The young man lowered himself in, and Rama followed. Pierre next and Herby hobbled through last.

✳ ✳ ✳ ✳ ✳ ✳

JALI'S EARS HAD monitored their progress up to the trapdoor, but he struggled to discern the chatter underground.

His attention returned to the truck. Beside him, Shiana bent low over the grass patch around her feet.

Siya tapped him. "Oh no, Prince. See, she's talking to herself again. What are you doing Shiana?"

"W-w-what are you l-l-looking at? I'll be fine here. You t-two go, go save Aka."

"Brelize will protect you," Jali said, leaving the red squirrel with her.

Without hesitation, he and Siya bolted to the fence to where the men had disappeared. They crawled under the barbed wire, and up the hill until they reached the exposed trapdoor. Jali lowered himself into a dark narrow tunnel.

Siya followed. "Where are you, Prince?"

Fireflies once again came to the rescue, brightening their way. "Come this way, Siya."

They tiptoed through the sinister burrow.

"Where are they? I can't hear them, Prince."

"I can hear them; they are this way." He skipped forward, his ears tuning in to the chatter up ahead. His Third Eye opened, and his ears perked as he caught his breath. "Hurry, Siya, something is wrong." He sprinted ahead, with the boy close behind.

A shot echoed through the tunnel.

His heart raced.

"Kri!" Herby's scream reverberated to them.

"Ay, no!" Siya shrieked.

The boys ran down the tunnel as fast as their feet could carry them.

"Kri!" Herby shouted again.

❇ ❇ ❇ ❇ ❇ ❇

CHAPTER THIRTEEN

The Great Escape

LIGHTS FLICKERED AT the end of the tunnel, which resounded with the boys' footsteps. Jali's ears perked. Angry words filled his head. *What are they saying?*

Iron clanked against stone as he emerged from the passageway and slid to a halt.

Where is everyone?

Walls towered around him, layered in endless levels, ablaze with petite fire lamps. Portraits of a beautiful woman, lined the stony walls, telling a story of woe. She wore a lost smile on her heart-shaped face, and in the wavering light, her blue eyes beckoned to be rescued.

Siya pulled on his arm. "This way, Prince."

The rattle of chains rippled to them, as they rushed through another narrow corridor, zipped around a corner, and ran across a horrific scene.

Against a gray stone wall, Rama struggled to free himself off thick iron chains shackling him to a giant pillar that rose high toward a glass dome. His screams muffled by a thick gag, his eyes rolled with rage.

Jali's Third Eye fluttered; it scanned the room and shut tight.

They were in a torture chamber. Women and men tied up like Rama hung throughout the hall. They were motionless.

Rama's nod directed the boys.

"This way," Jali yelled.

Siya followed him through a narrow passageway plastered with images of the mystical blonde, and through yet another opening.

Blinded by flashing lights, Jali shielded his eyes, and froze, unsure of what lay ahead. A stifled plea resonated from his right, where Herby struggled at a heavy door to a massive cage. He turned as Jali and Siya reached him.

"We must break this latch open, Prince!" He shouted, pulling frantically on a dead bolt.

They tugged at the door, in vain.

The doctor's bloodshot eyes pleaded for help. "Prince Jali, I must save Kri." He pointed, as lights from high above flashed onto a crumpled heap inside the cold, dark, stony cage.

Thunderous stomps loomed closer. "Oh, dear God, they're going to get us. Kri!"

Jali's heart thumped hard. He had to do something. Warmth crept up his spine. His Third Eye opened and scanned the cage.

I can do this. He closed his eyes, focused his Third Eye on the door, and took a deep breath. A picture of his mama and papa smiled at him. He let out his breath as his Third Eye projected an emerald laser, disintegrating the cage door. A ripple of energy shot through his tiny body, and he gasped before staggering. Siya grabbed him, and they both collapsed.

Herby rushed into the cage. "Kri, my love, don't worry, I'm gonna get you out of here." He moaned under her weight.

Siya rushed to his aid, and together they raised her.

Jali tottered off the icy floor, his energy rejuvenating with each step. They exited into the narrow passage as deafening trudges raced toward them. The trio ran as fast as they could, dragging Kriaka back through the tunnels, and returned to the chamber where Rama struggled against the chains.

Jali screeched to a halt beside him and shouted, "Go ahead, I shall meet you at the truck!"

Siya and Herby escaped with Kriaka through the tunnel entrance.

He ripped off Rama's gag.

"Look, kid, *go!*" Rama urged, his reddened eyes large. "Save yourselves. Kri and you are our only hope now kid. *Run!*"

Heavy clumps from the corridor were closing upon them.

Jali's ears perked and he hesitated.

❋ ❋ ❋ ❋ ❋ ❋

CHAPTER FOURTEEN

The Cloning Sword

JALI'S THIRD EYE scanned the knotted iron clad chains. He closed his two eyes and took in a deep breath. A familiar rush of warmth spread through his body and into his forehead, opening his Third Eye. An emerald beam surged, obliterating the shackles.

His tiny body drained once more, swayed and fell. Rama hauled him over his shoulder and they headed for the tunnel. Jali's ears perked. He peered over Rama's back. It was too late. Marching into the chamber, the Dragons surrounded them. A Dragon at the far end, dragged a bloodied and squirming Michael.

Behind the young man, a masculine voice boomed, rebounding every which way; louder and louder until the figure materialized in full view. Waves of darkness flowed around its tall lanky form, its head concealed by a dark hood. Long fingernails emerged out of its cloak and pointed at Rama.

"You dare enter my abode, and steal from me? Again!"

Jali's heart skipped a beat, and he felt Rama catch his breath.

"Rama, old chap, we meet once more!"

Jali felt Rama's grip on his legs tighten.

"This time you ensnared one of my very own for your selfish, nasty schemes," the thick voice drawled. "Not wise, old chap. This is my land, my country, my world! How dare you take my flesh and blood?"

Its voice battered Jali's ears shut. It circled them as Rama inched back.

Suddenly, hard, icy fingernails tilted Jali's head up from Rama's back. "Ho ho ho, what do we have here? Santa has arrived early!" The dark face, still indistinguishable from the shadows, puffed. "A three-eyed boy, who's been creating mischief in my world?"

It chuckled and commanded, "Set him down!"

Rama bent and lowered Jali, who couldn't stop shivering. "Look, Chan, this is between you and me. Let the kid go. He's just a little boy."

Chan laughed. "That's where it all starts, with little kids. See what you did to Michael?"

He beckoned his Dragons, and they hauled the

young man closer.

"What say you, my son?" Chan growled.

Michael replied in croaks. "Father, they made me bring them here. I'm loyal to you."

"He's loyal to me, did you hear that?" Chan said. He sneered.

The Dragons laughed. Chan reached under his cloak, raised a red whip, and cracked it toward them, grinding their laughter to a halt.

"Show me how loyal you are, my son. Here's your chance."

He rolled a glowing red sword toward Michael.

"Paralyze them. Start with the boy first. Then string him with the rest in the Cloning Chamber. Rama can watch what I do to my enemies." Chan glared at Rama. "I want you to feel what it's like to have the one you love torn from you." He paced around them. "She was mine. Mine. My Delight. But you, you couldn't let her go. No, not you, the great US engineer. Even when she promised to marry me, you had her in your clutches."

He looked up at the portrait that watched their every move, and waved his cloaked hands. "My beautiful Delight. If I couldn't have her, why should you? Do you know what it feels like to mute the one you love? I did it for her. So she could stop pining for you. She could belong to me once and for all."

Rama lunged into Chan. "You! You killed her! Why, Chan? Why? You married her, you had her. Jenniiii..." He fell to his knees, letting out a shrill scream.

"Cry, Rama, cry. I've never stopped crying, from the day I married her. She still had your name in her eyes, in her body, in the way she moved, in that musical voice. *You, you, you!*" He kicked Rama. "Now she can speak your name no more, she can desire you no more. But she *will* look at me, wherever I walk in this castle I built for her. I can have my Delight all to myself!

"Ha ha ha. Now the entire world must pay! See what you turned me into, Rama? All I wanted was to love and be loved. Now no one will love ever again! This planet will be mine."

He turned to Jali, whose heart jumped with fright.

"So, let's start with this three-eyed boy that you care about so much. Then we get Kriaka back. Clone her, so she can unlock the GIFT. Imagine that? I rule the worlds, and your lovely sister will be my companion!"

Rama tried to get up, but the Dragons jammed him down.

Chan neared Michael. "Son, let's see how loyal you are to me. Come on, time to show daddy what you're made of."

He motioned to his son and approached Jali, still curled on the ground. "Michael, come here!"

The young man refused to answer nor move, and the Dragons threw him across the floor.

Chan kicked the red sword to him.

"Here's the Cloning Sword. Into the boy's heart." He chuckled.

"Nooo!" Rama screamed and fought to break loose from the Dragons, in vain.

Shaking with fear, Jali tried to sit up and open his Third Eye, but failed. His body felt limp, his energy was depleted. Sinking to the floor, he watched helplessly.

Michael's head dripped sweat; a prominent twitch pulsed at the side of his neck. He frowned and bit his lower lip.

"*Son!*" Chan screamed. "Redeem yourself or die!"

"Yes, Father."

"Take it!"

Michael picked the fiery Cloning Sword and limped close to Jali's head.

"Don't do it," Rama pleaded. "You're not like him, you are different. Don't do it, Michael!"

Michael hesitated.

"*Son!*" Chan screamed.

As quick as lightning, Michael raised the Cloning Sword high.

Jali's heart froze, and he squeezed his eyes shut.

Rama screamed, "Noooooooooooooooooooo!"

The Cloning Sword plunged deep.

✳ ✳ ✳ ✳ ✳ ✳

CHAPTER FIFTEEN

The Impostor

JALI'S MAMA AND Papa smiled within a soft shower of flickering white lights.

He heard Rama scream. "Nooooooo!"

He saw the pointed Cloning Sword raised high in Michael's hand.

He felt the breeze from the swirl of luminous fire.

In one swoop, it was done.

Commotion exploded like a nuclear bomb.

Loud gasps echoed in the ghostly stone chamber.

Rama screamed incessantly and crawled into a ball of agony. Michael froze to the spot.

The Dragons stared...

The scene gradually cleared. All gazes fixed on the lustrous crimson glow shrouding its victim.

The Cloning Sword, deeply embedded in Chan's chest. A rosy shimmer danced around its clawed knob.

"Son, what have you done?" Chan groaned, reached to Michael, and lay motionless.

Jali's heart raced as Rama grabbed him. The ground shuddered. Rocks dropped off the walls and shards crashed from the glass dome.

An icy wind ripped through the castle, extinguishing every flicker of lamp light. A frightful moan echoed through the deathly darkness.

The blonde lady blinked her blue eyes.

In the sliver of star light from the shattered dome, Chan ascended. His head hung low on his chest. The Cloning Sword protruded from his body.

An evil and terrifying laughter usurped the blackened chamber, invading every hint of space.

"Ha, ha, ha! Like father, like son!" a familiar voice close to Chan said.

Chan continued to float to the open dome, unconscious.

As Jali's eyes adjusted to the dim light he caught his breath and shivered.

Supporting Chan's lifeless figure, was the man they knew as Pierre. Shadowy lights danced like puppets on his skeletal face; a lengthy dark cloak swelled around the horrific sight.

"You think you can defeat me? Think again!" he said, in a heavy ominous voice.

Jali swallowed hard. Rama, Michael, and the Dragons appeared frozen.

"We have the GIFT. I will return for your lovely Kriaka!"

He raised his elongated arm, masked under the dark robe, and pointed long curled fingernails at Jali.

"You, Prince Jali from planet Zooka, your Princess Reena will never ever enter my planet Earth. You, Prince, you will be mine. All mine to clone and rule the Cosmos by my side."

Jali felt faint.

Pierre let out a lethal laugh. "You and Kriaka and the GIFT. Imagine all we can do together. As one happy family!"

The cloak flowed around his menacing body, as he chuckled and shot through the dome, with Chan attached at his hip.

The terrified Dragons raced out of the chamber. Rama and Michael rooted, until Jali moaned.

Rama rushed to his side, and staggered from a heavy backdraft.

Jali whispered, "I am okay, Rama Adi." He pointed. "I think Michael needs your help."

Rama glanced back. The young man did not move.

Jali persisted, and Rama rushed to the frozen form, and tapped him. He jumped back, his eyes widened, his hair electrified in shock, his skin ghostly.

Rama patted him on the shoulder. "Look, come with us, time is short."

Michael blinked, nodded, and the trio raced into the last narrow tunnel and up through the open trapdoor.

Siya's hand reached down and guided Jali out. They hugged each other tight.

"Hayibo, we were worried; the whole ground was shaking! That cry, that cold—"

Rama cut in. "Quick, to the truck, we gotta get outta here *now*!"

They retraced their steps down the hill, under the fence and along the deserted way. When they reached Jen, Jali checked the backseats and sighed with relief. Herby leaned against Kri, held close by Shiana.

Rama jumped in. "Prince Jali, sit up front, I need you here."

Siya and Michael clambered behind them, and Jen screeched out of the long pathway. Jali hurled back in the seat as the truck lunged forward into the frightened night.

It was a straight road.

A long road.

Forsaken.

Numbed by darkness.

Jali's Third Eye fluttered. "Rama Adi, you should turn right and proceed through the pass."

Rama turned briefly to him. Then quickly agreed, making a sharp right turn back onto the dirt road. The screech of Jen's tires, desperate for a sign of sanctuary, smacked against pebbles, tiny boulders, and the occasional pothole.

✳ ✳ ✳ ✳ ✳ ✳

CHAPTER SIXTEEN

The Sacrifice

NOBODY SPOKE AND thirty minutes passed without a word.

A welcome quietness, until a loud gasp shattered the stillness.

Jali turned, as Siya switched on a light.

Kriaka's hand dripped blood.

Rama screamed. "Kri!"

He swerved the truck into the bushes. They jumped out, and he tore open the back door.

Herby slumped outward.

Rama caught him, and leaned him against his shoulders. Blood oozed out of the doctor's left side. He had been shot yet again!

Jali froze.

Kriaka moaned and reached for Herby.

Siya opened the medical bag, and Rama searched frantically for a treatment. "The blood, we must stop the blood," he said, his eyes bursting with panic. "Michael, press on it."

He pressed while Rama unrolled a swathe of bandages from the bag.

Jali watched in horror, his heart thumping against his ribs.

Herby reached for Kriaka's face and whispered her name.

"Herb, my love." She stroked his face and ran her fingers through his damp blond hair.

"You'll be okay, Kri."

Shiana knelt at her side and cried. "Herby, n-n-no, don't leave us, Herby, don't leave us."

She got up and rushed over to Jali, who looked on in shock. "P-P-Prince, save him, Prince, save him. I know you can. Save him, Prince. You must s-save him." She tugged at his arm, imploring.

Desperate gazes locked onto Jali. His breath accelerated as a recent scene flashed past his eyes. *Reena had recharged Grandma in the Royal Garden.*

Rama and Michael moved aside, and he stooped at the doctor's side. Placing both hands on Herby's shoulders, he closed his eyes and took in a deep breath. A warmth crept up his Third Eye. It fluttered, and letting out his breath, he focused.

He waited.

And waited.

Everyone waited.

Nothing.

"Time to let me go, my little Prince Jali."

He cringed.

The doctor looked at Kriaka. "Remember our dream, my Kri?"

She smiled and caressed his face; his blue eyes sparkled.

"Make it happen, my love, my dearest Angel. The world is depending on you. For now, our Dove awaits me."

Herby smiled at Jali, and closed his eyes.

Kriaka rocked the doctor like a baby. Tears streamed down her bruised face.

Each and every one looked on, stunned.

Rama placed his fingers on the doctor's neck. He pursed his lips, and shook his head. For several minutes, he knelt beside Herby's limp body, and nobody moved.

Rama stood tall.

He paced back and forth.

With force, he crushed his fist into the roof of the truck, and in slow motion slumped to the grass.

Clasping his head, he sobbed.

✳ ✳ ✳ ✳ ✳ ✳

CHAPTER SEVENTEEN

Ghosts and Spirits

A VACUUM OF SILENCE swept through the African forest. Every leaf, every flower, every petal, and every pollen pod retracted into a space of nonbeing.

Unending.

Until an orange-breasted sunbird chirped and alighted on Jali's hand.

He stroked its tiny bopping head.

High above, the Dove twinkled intensely, reflecting against Siya and Shiana's wet faces.

Michael leaned on the open door, his gaze frozen on the couple in the backseat.

Rama, his body fastened against Jen's tire, sat rock-still on the grass.

White butterflies gathered over Jen and fireflies haloed Herby and Kriaka. Countless suns bejeweled the evening sky.

A strange hollow crept into the pit of Jali's body. He gasped for breath, and his eyes welled. He left the devastation. He wrapped his arms around the wide trunk of an uSolu tree, and sobbed.

I could not save Doctor Herby! The kind, sweet Doctor who saved me. I could not save him. I thought Michael was the Impostor. I trusted Pierre. My superpowers failed me. I am useless.

He had never before felt so utterly alone and abandoned. Not even Brelize's furry paw against his cheek could ease the unbearable grief lodged within him.

After a few moments, a hand rested on his shoulder.

"Prince, are you okay?" Siya asked.

"Siya, I failed to save Doctor Herby."

"I think Doc was hurt bad. I don't think you could've helped him. He knew that." The boy patted Jali's back. "You helped Herby survive the first bullet. You released Kriaka's cage. You rescued Rama."

Siya whispered, in between soft sobs. "Hope is not lost. Wise One says the good never die in vain.

"Kriaka can help to bring Princess Reena and your Zookian warriors to us and save those of us who are left behind."

Jali held on to his Earth friend and cried.

Gradually he calmed. *The good never die in vain.*

He sighed long and slow. *Yes, Kriaka Adi will direct us to Mont Aux Sources. I shall beam to Zooble, and Reena, Commander ZW1, and the Magnificent ZW7 warriors will save Shiana, Siya, Rama, Michael, Wise One, Majestic One, Brelize, and all the pure beings.*

Brelize scurried up his arm and into his Earth-boy hood. Feeling more assured, he followed Siya back to Jen.

At the truck, Rama and Michael wrapped blankets around Herby's bloodied body, and they gently placed him in the space behind Kriaka's seat. She sat still, her waist encircled by Shiana's protective arms.

Rama spoke softly. "Sis?"

Kriaka looked at him with glazed eyes. He gathered her close and stroked her head.

"We're going to make it, Kri. Just as you and Herby dreamed. We're gonna do it, Sis."

She blinked without saying a word. Her arms limp at her side.

Rama touched her face. "She's ice-cold. Siya, get the blankets."

The boy raced to the back of the truck, bringing back Kriaka's favorite blankets. Rama wrapped her and rubbed her arms. "Siya, Shiana, keep her warm." He kissed her head and shut the door.

Jali took up his seat beside Rama. Michael poked his head between them, and spoke for the first time since the tragic scene at the castle. "She doesn't look right."

Rama bit his lip. "She's in shock. She just needs to rest."

They drove hushed, and every few minutes Rama craned his neck to check on Kriaka. He sighed each time.

Close on the hour, Jali's Third Eye fluttered. "Rama Adi, up ahead is a village where Wise One's relatives are waiting for us."

Rama glanced at him and raised his eyebrows. He nodded and they bumped along the dirt road. In the distance, a glow caught their attention.

As they approached, blazing fires atop long sticks, held by hundreds of tribal men, women, and children, lined their path. Rama drove amid a deep hum. At the end of the pathway, three men greeted them and spoke to Jali in rushed tones.

"What are they saying?" Rama asked.

"They have been waiting for us, Rama Adi," Jali replied. "The tribal village has prepared a royal burial for Doctor Herby."

✳ ✳ ✳ ✳ ✳ ✳

MINI FIRES BRIGHTENED the tiny umuzi village.

In the center, Herby's body lay on a raised wooden bed topped with white roses. Children danced around him, led by Siya. Kriaka held her father's blanket tight.

Shiana supported her on one side and Rama on the other, as they stood at the doctor's feet.

Shrill cries of the tribal villagers rent the clear moonlit sky. A falling star trailed a blissful afterglow. Majestic One reached to Jali, and he joined the villagers in the traditional tribal dance.

A deep hum resonated throughout the Draco mountains and forests as the Dove constellation gleamed on Doctor Herby.

✸ ✸ ✸ ✸ ✸ ✸

CHAPTER EIGHTEEN

Amnesia

RAMA SAT WITHOUT Herby.

He cradled Kriaka while Shiana slept soundly at her side. Plates of food lay untouched on stone tables inside the still hut.

Jali felt lost without the kind blue-eyed doctor, and he huddled close to Siya, for comfort. Brelize curled at their feet.

Michael paced up and down, ducking his head now and then under the protruding straws in the coned ceiling. "Something is not right!" he said. "I knew that my father was developing evil powers. But I didn't know about the scale of his operation."

He struck his palm against his forehead. "And that thing!" His eyes widened. "I thought Pierre was with you guys! I suspected something when he accused me of kidnapping Kriaka. I was nowhere near there, and I know that the Dragons didn't take her either!"

Rama looked up sharply. "Shoot, it all makes sense. Pierre could be Chan's main clone with supernatural powers. He could be planning his attack on us right now." He lowered his voice. "Sis, we must plan our route for the morning. Kri?"

She did not move. She did not reply. She stared at the ground.

Michael scratched his head. "I told you, she hasn't moved much or said anything since Herby died!"

"Kri?" Rama repeated.

Footsteps neared the entrance, and Majestic One ducked his feathered head and entered. "I'm so sorry about the Doctor. He was a good man."

Rama nodded before Majestic One filled them in. "Wise One instructed me to escort you to Mont Aux Sources. You need word sent out to the First Ones?"

"Yes," Rama replied. "Only Kriaka knows the location of the Portal at Mont Aux Sources, but she is in a state of shock."

"You are right. Wise One says that your sister holds the key to opening the Gateway before the Portal." Majestic One glanced at Kriaka and continued. "You know I've seen this type of shock. For some, it takes a few

<del>105</del>

weeks to recover."

Jali's heart raced. *Weeks?*

"We don't have weeks!" Michael said, in a panicked voice. "What are we going to do? We're doomed!"

Rama coughed. "Okay, let's rest up and see what happens in the morning, when we're all thinking clearly."

He carried Shiana to the hammock in the corner of the hut and guided Kriaka to the girl. He kissed their heads and Jali joined him and the men outside the hut.

"This may be the last few days of our lives!" Michael rested his hand on Siya's shoulder. They headed to a roaring fire, circled with the villagers.

Jali and Rama remained outside the hut.

"I've known Herb since childhood," Rama said as they sat on the grass. "Our parents were the best of friends. They led the underground resistance against the Dragons. When the fight roughed up, they bundled me off to the US 'cos I was getting out of control. Good ol' Herb, the dependable one, he stayed with the folks. I got a note from him one day, saying that something was going down. I came back. That's when we sent Kri to the US for safekeeping. Herby and I, we rekindled our brotherly bond. Ten years later, our parents were executed. Our Kri came home, and I could tell that he was in love with her. He always said that Kri fell for his devastating blue eyes and boyish blond hair."

Jali stifled a sob.

Rama patted his shoulders. "You did what you could, kid. Prince Jali. I'm sorry I didn't believe you." He draped his arm around him and pulled him close. "I'm honored to have met you. You saved my life today. You saved Kri. Because of you, Herby was able to get Kri out."

His voice cracked, he rose and entered the hut.

Jali wiped the tears from his face. Up in the Cosmos the Dove twinkled.

Reena, why could I not save Doctor Herby? He was a pure being. Why did he have to die?

Siya interrupted his thoughts, and sat with him in silence, staring at the night sky.

Over time, the orphaned boys snuggled together, with Brelize at their feet, and nodded off to sleep.

✳ ✳ ✳ ✳ ✳ ✳

CHAPTER NINETEEN

Apocalypse Prophecy

Third morning

THE MORNING SUN peeled away the night's gloom. Streaks of orange splashed across the brilliant cloudless sky. Jali had recharged under a thick tribal blanket all through the short night. Next to him, Siya lay curled in his own blanket.

Without disturbing the boy, he tiptoed and entered the hut. Rama sat at the edge of the hammock, watching over Kriaka. Shiana stretched and rose softly.

Soon, the tribal village bustled with activity. Shiana ate breakfast with Siya, Brelize and Jali, and every now and then she picked up a grain of sand, whispered something, and set it down again. Close by, Michael and Majestic One chatted in low tones.

Rama emerged from the hut with Kriaka. "Shiana,

show Kri where to wash up." The girl ran with excitement to Kriaka, threaded her hand into hers, and guided her slender figure to the tribal women farther in the village.

Rama, Siya, and Jali joined Michael and Majestic One to discuss the coordinates to Mont Aux Sources and the Portal.

The African leader unfolded a crinkled map onto the ground.

"This is the original map of the mountain passes." He pointed to several spots on the worn paper. "No other map shows the hundreds of hidden routes and caves in this Draco area."

The men were pouring over the markings, when Shiana returned with Kriaka.

"Sis, grab a bite to eat, we need our energy today, okay?" Rama said.

But there was no response, and he frowned as they watched Shiana take her to the breakfast spread under the tree.

Majestic One patted him. "The imprisonment plus the shock of losing the doctor could have triggered regression."

Michael paced up and down. "Oh man, what are we going to do?"

"Wise One said that she could recover at anytime when supported with pure love."

Rama's voice brightened with hope. "Kri is constantly surrounded by love. We grew up together, she is loved by Shiana and Siya. And she adores Prince Jali. I'm convinced we can jog her memory and bring her mind back home where she belongs."

He looked lovingly at Kriaka sitting motionless next to Shiana.

Jali's heart sank. *What if the Impostor has Kriaka's mind?* He motioned to Siya, and they wandered through the tribal village, with Brelize at their heels.

"What if Chan and his Pierre find us before Kriaka's memory returns?" Jali whispered.

Siya placed his hands on either side of his head and rolled his eyes. "Hayibo, then the prophecy will come true."

"Prophecy?"

"Ycbo, it has been said that when people become so evil that they hurt each other for power, lust, or greed, and they destroy nature, then life and all time will disappear."

Jali's ears perked and he listened with intent.

"Only one person in the tribe is aware of the day of doom, the Apocalypse."

"Wise One?"

"Yebo, she's the one."

"When is the end of time?"

"Ay, we're not to know that. It's better this way."

Siya tugged at him and pulled him behind a hut. He looked around. "Hayibo, I have not seen this type of help before. You know, when all the races come together. When Majestic One steps forward to help, it means that Wise One has warned him. Yebo, I think we are in the time just before the Apocalypse. The end of time is close, Prince."

Jali's heart took a dip, and he bit his lip.

But Siya smiled and shrugged. "Yebo, I'm happy that I got to know you." The boy's smile quickly vanished. "But you know what is the pity?"

"What, Siya?"

"The pity is that you come from the place we all wish we lived in. Utopia. But you come here, and get stranded here. Stuck here, and if things don't work out, ay, you will die here. Hayibo, not good. Prince from Utopia dies on corrupt planet Earth!"

Jali felt as if he had been punched hard in his stomach, like on his first day. His heart palpitated. *Oh no! What if Siya is right?*

He grabbed the boy. "Come, I shall summon Reena."

He pulled him into a bush behind the elder's hut.

"Hey, Prince, that will drain your energy."

"There is a question I must have answered," Jali insisted.

Siya gave in. He looked around and gave the okay signal, a thumbs-up while Brelize stood guard, her long tail stiff.

Jali shut his eyes, focused his recharged energy, and opened his Third Eye. A blue light spiraled in front of them.

The Zookian Glass appeared with Commander ZW1 and Reena in the Control Chamber, each with a serious face.

"Greetings, Jee. Much has happened since we last spoke. Know even though we are observing each occurrence, we are still unable to intervene, even in life threatening situations, like the one you were in with Chan. We are thankful that Michael saved your life," Reena said.

Commander ZW1 spoke. "Prince Jali, the disturbing vibrations around this planet interfere with the full potency of your Third Eye powers. We have realized that your powers can work a maximum of three times a day if used in small capacities, or once if the positive energy is depleted. Whichever comes first."

"Jee, remember, each time you call on the Zookian Glass, half your positive energy drains."

Jali interrupted her with his pressing questions. "Reena, why couldn't I save Doctor Herby? I loved him so much!"

"Jee, you are not to alter what is supposed to happen on this planet. Grandma says that Herby was to pass on at that time. Remember, the good ones never die in vain. What we must focus on, is to retrieve the GIFT so that Kriaka Adi proceeds with her plan to rescue the pure beings. This is our mission. But first, we must extricate you before you fall into the hands of the Impostor. If we fail, the future will change for the worse and time will stop. You must rekindle Kriaka Adi's memory, and align with the Portal in *seventy-two Earth hours*. Grandma gets weaker each day you are away. Jee, time is short..."

The transmission became weaker and faded.

"I love you, Reena. Tell Grandma I will make her better," Jali whispered, before sinking from exhaustion.

Siya grabbed him and lowered him to the ground.

"Grandma!"

"Prince Jali, you love your Grandma much."

"Yes, she cannot die. She is weakened because I have not returned to Zooble. It has something to do with the future and time. Which I cannot understand."

Shiana jumped out from the bushes, startling them and Brelize.

"P-P-Prince, I think I know where Tuttles is," she whispered with joy.

"Where?" He bubbled with joy, unable to contain his thrill.

"They s-s-said he is 'where the sun don't shine.'"

"Hayibo, Shiana, that's a bad thing to say." Siya said, covering his ears with his hands.

"B-b-but, Siya, that's what the ants s-said."

She pursed her lips and strung out the words one at a time.

"Yes, where... the... sun... don't... really... shine."

"Really shine?" the boys repeated, cocking their heads.

"Prince Jali, Siya, Shiana, get ready, we leave soon," Rama hollered from the front of the hut.

❋ ❋ ❋ ❋ ❋ ❋

CHAPTER TWENTY

The GIFT

THE YOUNGSTERS RUSHED to Jen, and they found a troop of eight open trucks filled with tribal warriors, whose faces were painted fiery red.

Majestic One grinned with pride. "Yes, we have some troops now, Prince Jali." The village leader looked at Rama and shrugged. "I'm afraid we don't have enough. But the word is out, and we can expect more."

Next to Rama, Michael updated the prince. "I may know how to find out where the GIFT is."

He set forth to clarify his words to the amazed Jali. Michael explained that before the infected machines were destroyed fifty years back, a substantial top-secret nanochip was relocated, together with a supercomputer called the Accumulated Intelligence Core, the AIC. His father had negotiated for its purchase over ten years ago. Today, Michael intended to access the AIC and use it to locate the GIFT. Junior, Majestic One's son, would escort him to the underground location in Spioenkop, north east of them.

"I know lots about the old computers. I can help!" Siya chimed in.

Michael welcomed his assistance, and they joined Junior in the first truck, speeding off in hope that by locating the GIFT, Kriaka's memory would return.

Jali felt hopeful, but his joy was replaced by a pang of sadness. The time had arrived for Jen to continue her journey to Mont Aux Sources, but without the doctor. He sighed as he and Shiana settled into the backseat. Rama guided Kriaka to the front, and revved Jen into action, and the villagers waved.

Jen followed Majestic One's expansive open truck packed with armed tribal warriors.

Five similar trucks tailed Jen, sparking a sense of security in Jali.

A short while into their drive, Rama turned to him. "Prince Jali, tell us about where you come from?"

He smiled. Rama, just like each of them, was determined to cheer Kriaka and jog her back to reality.

With great excitement, he described Zooka, Reena, Grandma, Brela, Tuttles, their pure food, clean water and air, and their love for all life forms and peace throughout the Cosmos.

Rama clapped his hand on the dashboard. "You hear that, Kri? This is just the place you've been describing ever since you were little. Utopia *does* exist!"

But she remained silent beside him.

Shiana bumped Jali, her eyes seeming to fill with wonder. "And t-t-tell us about Tuttles?"

He sighed and lowered his voice. "I was to fly after I graduated on my fourteenth birthday this year. But for some reason, each time I tried, I was unable to fly."

"Fly?" Shiana shrieked with delight, sending Brelize back into Jali's Earth-boy hood.

"Sure, everyone can fly on Zooka."

Rama chuckled. "So there are no cars or trucks or planes?"

"No, everything is powered by our natural powers. We promise to use our own abilities for everything and do not create objects that harm any life form. We do not injure the sand, air, water, flora, or fauna because they are essential life forms, just like us."

"So, what is Tuttles?" Rama asked.

His prompt was all Jali needed to talk about his best friend. "Because I was unable to fly, my friend Tuttles suggested that I practice my Third Eye superpowers on him. I did, and we became invisible when I rode on him.

But it does not last too long, and we cannot fly too high."

"Fly! Invisible!" Rama caressed Kriaka's cheek. "Kri, that's what you will love!" His eyes glistened as he held her hand.

"B-b-but Tuttles came with Prince, but he is missing."

"Missing?" Rama said.

"Yes, Reena says he is not on Zooble," Jali said.

"B-b-but the ants told me that Tuttles is waiting where the sun doesn't really shine."

Jali shrugged and whispered in a sad tone, "And we do not know where that is."

The thought of not finding Tuttles, saddened him. *Where are you my friend. Do not worry, I shall find you.* Brelize curled her tail around his wrist. He smiled, thankful for her presence.

The travelers journeyed in silence, and focused their attention on the truck ahead of them, as they winded their way through the rugged trails, flanked by towering mountains.

Two hours into the journey, the troop stopped along a cluster of trees, to coordinate their plans. The men gathered at the lead truck, their necks bent over the treasured Draco map.

Around them the magnificent treeless mountains rose high, and beneath, its abundant forests livened with smells and sounds similar to Zooka.

As Jali sighed with longing for home, a creaking door disrupted his thoughts, and he gasped.

Kriaka was reaching into his open window. She placed a small shimmering object in his palm and closed his fingers over. With the angelic smile he had come to know so well, she returned to her seat, and the door creaked shut.

Brelize clambered on his shoulder eager for for a peek, and Shiana tugged at his arm unable to contain her curiosity. "W-w-what is it? What did Aka give you?"

He looked at the glistening gift in his palm and shrugged in confusion.

"Th-th-that's it!" Shiana said with a gleeful smile, and jumped out, dragging Jali with her.

✳ ✳ ✳ ✳ ✳ ✳

End Of Book ii: ꝺïKónå

Taming The Impostor Saga
Adventure Time Travel Fantasy Series

For the young at heart

Read On

Paperback, eBooks and AudioBooks

Book i: Dance of Fireflies

Book ii: ꝺïKónå

Book iii: Wuñamångåz

The Pure Ones Books i-iii

SPECIAL GIFTS FOR YOU

I hope you enjoyed ﾑîḰóǹǎ Book ii in Taming The Impostor Saga Fantasy Adventure.

I'd love for you to **Leave Your Review**.

☆☆☆

If after you leave your review, you would like to **join my VIP ARC Team of Readers** for upcoming books, go here:

www.DrVie.com/ARC-Team

☆☆☆

Want To Know More About The Series?

Go to www.DrVie.com/ Taming-The-Impostor-map

FREE SHORT STORY FOR YOU

DrVie.com/VIPfreebooks

Prequel to Taming The Impostor Saga

❇ ❇ ❇ ❇ ❇ ❇

CONNECT WITH ME

Say hello or let me know how I can be of help to you and
loved ones.

www.DrVie.com (main site)
www.facebook.com/ScientistDoctorVie
www.twitter.com/DrVie
www.Youtube.com/DrVieSuperfoods
www.Instagram.com/Doctor.Vie

✲✲✲

Enjoy more EBooks, AudioBooks and Paperbacks:
Taming The Impostor Saga
Book i: Ɗance of ƒiƦeƒliȩş
Book ii: ⱭïҚóñå
Book iii ѠųñamåñɠɅz
Ɀhe puƦe Ones Books i-iii

✲✲✲

I thank you for your support which helps me mentor
thousands of youth for free through my global Super-
Conscious Humanity Youth Program

❋ ❋ ❋ ❋ ❋ ❋

ABOUT DR. SHERI VIE

My dear Reader,

Life sure is an adventure, even with family and friends.

For me, my youthful adventures really began solo when I left South Africa to study in the USA-certainly uncommon in those days, for a single Indian female.

Since then, I've been living in six countries, twenty plus cities...on my own. A real-life adventure; new places, a variety of people, numerous cultures, exotic foods, foreign languages and of course endless challenges.

What truly amazed me beyond the fascinating cities, towns and traditions, were the breathtaking natural environments as I hiked high up in the mountain trails around the globe, sometimes with a guide and most often on my own. The African ranges to the Himalayan peaks. Pristine air, sounds of nature, and the splendor of fauna and flora in their natural habitat resonated with me. Staring into the eyes of a young deer, strolling adjacent alongside a giraffe, and reveling in the dainty clasp of a humming bird on my finger.

When I'm not exploring mountains, I share stories of my adventures to tens of thousands of all ages, from tiny tots to the 100+, in poverty stricken villages to plush halls. What a joy to witness their personal transformations. I love inspiring our fellow humans.

My rewards come from the excitement in their eyes, the smiles that fill their faces, and the abundant hugs after each session.

My work is my personal journey, and I live a simple life, pouring any revenue back into my volunteer work around the globe.

Now, I share many of the adventurous stories through my writings tinged with fantasy. I'd love for you to explore my books and send me your thoughts and feedback. It's a small world bounding with adventure, and I would love to hear yours.

Lots of love, and hugs, always, V.

❋ ❋ ❋ ❋ ❋ ❋

CHARACTERS ON UTOPIAN PLANET ZOOKA

Books i and ii

Brela (Jali's Zookian squirrel friend)

Commander ZW1 (Chief of the Peace-Keeping Force)

Elder Lion (Zookian)

Green Tortoise (Zookian)

Guardian 1 (Jali's Teacher)

Jali (Reen'as brother, Queen Vraka's grandson)

Jee (Reena's nick name for Jali)

Mama (Jali's & Reena's mother)

Magnificent ZW7 (Zookian special warriors)

Papa (Jali's & Reena's father)

Peace-Keeping Force (Cosmic Peace Keepers)

Prince Jali (Reena's brother)

Princess Reena (Jali's sister, Queen Vraka's granddaughter)

Protector 1 (Queen Vraka's Advisor)

Queen Vraka (Jali & Reena's Grandma, Queen of Zooka)

Reena (Jali's sister, Queen Vraka's granddaughter)

Tuttles (Jali's Zookian turtle friend)

✳ ✳ ✳ ✳ ✳ ✳

CHARACTERS ON APOCALYPTIC PLANET EARTH

Books i and ii

Big Boss (supervisor of African warriors)

Brelize (Jali's squirrel Earth friend)

Chan (Michael's father, Dragon leader)

Dragons (Chan's evil gang)

First Ones (pure beings)

Herby (doctor, Doctor Jekyll, Kriaka's fiance)

Ivan (Dragon)

Junior (son of Majestic One)

Kriaka Adi (leader of First Ones, Brown Witch)

Kri (Kriaka's pet name)

Meosic (Shiana's sand cat)

Majestic One (African tribal leader)

Michael (Chan's son)

Miss Amber (school teacher)

Pierre (supposed follower?)

Rama Adi (Mr. Hyde, Kriaka's brother, previous leader of First Ones)

Saks (Dragon)

Shiana (Ana, Kriaka's sister)

Siya (Shiana's friend)

Tribal Teacher (African teacher)

Vincent (Siya's brother)

Wise One (mystical African elder)

✳ ✳ ✳ ✳ ✳ ✳

WORLD ON UTOPIAN PLANET ZOOKA

Books i and ii

Control Chamber (in Zooble)

Cosmo 13

Cosmos

Field of Detection

Force-1 Shield

Galaxy Al86

Level-4 (Graduation level)

Level-5 (Graduation level)

Lotus Wand (Queen Vraka's ancient spear)

Magical Arrows of Power (Princess Reena's weapons)

Magnificent ZW7 (Zookian special warriors)

Peace-Keeping Force

P1 invisible shield

planet Zooka

Royal Bed

Royal Cave

Royal (Counsel) Chamber

Royal Garden

Royal Guardian

Royal Observation Chamber

Royal Zooble Chamber

Spear of V (Princess Reena's weapon)

Summit (hideout to watch Zooble Dome)

Sword of Khadga (Princess Reena's weapon)

Telepathy (communicate via thoughts)

Third Eye (super-conscious powers)

Transporter (to beam over/to cross over)

Utopia (perfect place)

Z-Clock

Z-days

Z-seconds

Zarp-speed

Zooble Dome (lift off deck for space ships)

Zooble intergalactic space explorer

Zooka (planet)

Zookian (life-form)

Zookian Glass (hologram communicator)

Zookian Locator (detect intergalactic places)

Zookian-months

Zookish (language on Zooka)

✳ ✳ ✳ ✳ ✳ ✳

WORLD ON APOCALYPTIC PLANET EARTH

Books i and ii

Africa (continent)

Arena Park (town in Chatsworth)

Basotho Land (country adjacent South Africa)

Cathedral Peak (mountain area)

Champagne Valley (mountain area)

Chatsworth (area in Kwa-Zulu Natal)

Dark Force Two (Impostor)

Draco (Dragon mountain)

Drakensberg (mountain range)

First Ones (Kriaka's pure team)

Giant's Castle (mountain area in Drakensberg)

Gateway (first opening to Portal)

GIFT (mysterious stone)

Jen (bakkie, Rama's truck)

KwaZulu-Natal (eastern province of South Africa)

laanis (rich ones)

Mercedes (fancy car)

Milky Way

Monks Cowl (mountain range)

Mooi River (town)

Mont Aux Sources (mountain at the source)

planet Earth

Portal

rainbow nation (united in diversity)

South Africa (country on continent of Africa)

Unit 1 (township area in Chatsworth)

Umlazi (Black township)
Umuzi (Zulu village)
uSolu (the great African shade tree)
Winterton (town east of the Draco mountains)
Zulu (African language)

✳ ✳ ✳ ✳ ✳ ✳

DISCOVERING NEW LANGUAGES

Aikona (no)

Andromeda (galaxy near Milky Way)

bakkie (jeep)

bru (slang for brother)

Canis Major (constellation)

Columba the Dove (constellation)

duffle bag (soft carrying bag)

Earth-boy hood (hood of jacket)

ethalion (butterflies)

ho (slang for man/guy)

Ja (Dutch term for yes)

lammergeyer (vulture)

Lepus the Hare (constellation)

muthi (tribal medicine)

Orion Nebula (constellation)

petrol (gasoline, gas)

smaak (Dutch term for like)

strelitzia (bird/beaked plant)

umuzi (circular settlement/kraal)

uSolu (shade tree)

Zulu (African language in South Africa)

My Notes